Loving a Married Man

May be Hazardous to Your Health

Kaylynn Thomas

This book is dedicated to the ones I love, My children—my always, my everything, my world: Darrell Sr., George Jr., Monique, Kevin Sr., and Damian Sr.

I also dedicate this book to my mother, Shirley Thompson Merrick, the greatest woman I have ever known. There's no other like you. I love you, mom.

Please keep in mind: I am not a professional writer. My work is partially fiction, well, mostly fiction. Names and places are also fiction, mostly. And, in no way am I throwing shade at anyone, living or dead. It's not about you!

Acknowledgments:
I'm sending a special thanks to myself
because I believed in me.

WHEN HE WALKS IN A ROOM A LIGHT SEEMS TO GLOW, HIS SMILE IS AN ADDED CHARM. MY HEART GOES INTO A FRENZY OF BEATS BUT, HE IS IN SOMEONE ELSE'S ARMS.

I was raised to respect the sanctity of marriage. "What God had joined together; no man nor woman shall come amid." That's what my mother used to say.

My mother had repeatedly pressed to my sister, Joni, and I that seeing a married man makes you his number two. My mother did not raise her daughters to become anyone's number two.

In spite of my mother's teachings, I fell in love with a married man. It was damaging to my heart when I learned that he was married; still, I found it hard to let go of that male phenomenon.

Through the eyes of God and by the laws of man, I had become a number two. He had conjured his spell, and I fell hopelessly under his curse as a willing participant.

My name is Victoria Thompson, and this is my story.

Loving a Married Man

KAYLYNN THOMAS

****

Michael Duncan, New Orleans leading cancer researcher, was in the merriest of moods. He had finally decided to leave his wife to be with the secret love that he had kept hidden for nearly a decade.

It was almost ten years ago when Michael first laid eyes on the love of his life. One day, while walking home, he passed a *Save the Planet Rally* held in Louis Armstrong Park. Standing near the stage, he saw, who he thought, was the most beautiful woman in the world.

She had a smile that could melt the heart of a mortal man, and she had the most amazing eyes. Michael had never seen eyes like that on a woman of her color. Just the sight of her stirred something in him. A stir he had never known.

He was immediately smitten with her and could not turn away his gaze. He headed towards her to introduce himself. As he fought his way through the ocean of spectators, she had vanished.

Loving a Married Man

Ever since Michael would take the scenic route home, he would pass Armstrong Park daily, hoping to see her again. Months had passed and still no sign of her. He was beginning to think maybe she was a figment of his imagination.

While Michael was walking home one evening, he passed a coffee shop called "LaDelle's." He had heard outstanding reviews about the place and had been meaning to visit for a cappuccino. *Why not today?* He thought.

Michael entered the shop and, the aroma of freshly brewed coffee proved to be pleasant to his senses. He seated himself by the window so he could watch the passerby's and play his little game he had invented, *drown or save.*

He would pretend each person passing was drowning and, he would choose which ones to save and which ones to let drown. 'Drown, drown, save, drown, save, save, save, drown.'

When the waitress approached his

table, she could hear him say drown, save and, looked at him cautiously. She interrupted his little game by clearing her throat.

When Michael turned to give her his order, his heart skipped a beat. There she was, the woman, who at one glance, had stolen his heart, was now waiting to serve him coffee. He wasn't about to let her get away again. Her name tag read Shirley. *What a beautiful name*, he thought to himself.

It wasn't long before they began to spend every spare moment together. Michael had purchased an apartment for her. It was a place where they could be free to express their feelings for each other.

As the years passed, Michael grew restless, having to keep her a secret. She grew restless, having to *be* a secret.

Michael had made up his mind that he would no longer hide her in the shadows or keep up the appearance for the sake of his career. He was going to be free to be with the woman he adored.

Loving a Married Man

On the walk to her apartment, he felt a twinge in his chest. He thought it was because of the excitement of finally being able to be with the woman he loved, so he ignored the twinge.

As he entered her apartment, carrying a dozen long-stemmed red roses and an engagement ring in his pocket, he clutched his chest and fell to the floor.

"Michael!" the woman cried out as she ran to his aid. "Baby, what is wrong?" she asked, kneeling beside him, lifting him in her arms.

Michael was sadly looking at the woman he loved and knew at that moment that would be the last time he would have the pleasure of gazing upon her ebony beauty. Michael had died…

CHAPTER ONE

My sister, Joni, and I never had the pleasure of meeting our father, and our mother would never talk about him.

Whenever we tried to have a conversation about the absentee sperm donor, it made our mother cry, and she was sad for days. So, we figured it was best to leave it alone.

My mother never gossiped, and whenever she would walk upon us gossiping, she would point out our inadequacies and then explain why she did it. She would tell us that we were not perfect, so how could we speak badly of someone else?

Loving a Married Man

Joni was the good daughter and mimicked my mother. I was the total opposite. The black sheep–the demon seed–the spawn from hell–a diablo. I was always getting into trouble and getting Joni grounded for just being with me.

Anyway, every Sunday morning, our mother dragged us to church to instill Christian values in us. Well, just me, Joni innately had them. On Thursday nights, she dragged us to choir practice. Maybe *drag* is a bit harsh, but *dragged* is what she did.

My mother taught us to accept and respect the differences in others. That was her way of telling us to accept people for whom and what they were. That was not always easily done.

Our mother was a true-blooded, heaven-spawned Christian, not a wolf or demon in Christian clothing; you know the kind. She lived by and honored God's Commandments. We called our mother a "beautiful goddess" because she was always so beautiful and god-like.

Whenever we would call her beautiful, she would tell us that beauty was only skin-deep. Meaning, looks did not mean a thing. I could not figure out why she would say something like that when everyone knows an image is everything. Joni agreed with my mom that looks did not matter.

I said bullshit! Looks matter! If looks were not so important, why would anyone pay image counselors thousands of dollars to make them *look* a certain way?

Let me give you an example. Let's say two young men are walking down the street, one boy on each side of the street.

One of them is wearing his pants below the equator and has on a hoodie. You would think hood, right? Murderer, right? Gangster, right? He is in his third year of college.

Now, the other young man is dressed nicely in a shirt and tie. You would think a nice young man, right? Educated, right? Trustworthy, right? But he just killed several people.

Now ask yourself what side of the street you would walk on. You would walk on the side of the murderer because he *looked* safer. Get my point?

For those of you that believe looks do not matter, deliberate again. Why do we get our hair and our nails done, wear makeup, and wear expensive or trendy clothes? It is to portray a certain image.

Besides that, why are plastic surgeons filthy rich? To make us pretty or handsome. Because *we* as human beings are VAIN and SHALLOW as hell! Image/looks, whatever. No one cares what is inside your head or heart. Thus, *looks* matters.

CHAPTER 2

Getting back to dragging us to church. It was not that our mother had to drag us, it was just that our church was so early and lasted so long on Sunday mornings. It was hard getting out of bed after a mischievous Saturday night.

And choir practice lasted so long on Thursday nights. We had school to attend the next day. Many a Friday morning, I slept through my first period.

Despite it all, we enjoyed going to church because it pleased our mother. But mostly, we enjoyed going to school to get away from our mother.

High school was where we learned about sex, how to *French* kiss, how to smoke, how to cut class, and how to change our report-card grades.

We learned how to hot-wire a car and how to forge our mother's signature on documents we knew she would never sign. High school was so educational.

We also learned, boys can be jerks and girls can be extremely mean.

Charlotte, the bitch, was one of the mean girls (remember her) that used to rag on me a lot.

Charlotte's parents had mega-money, so she also had money. She dressed better than me (meaning her clothes were more expensive), and her status was on a larger scale than mine.

Yet, there was something about me that had erupted that ever-so-infamous green-eyed monster in her. Hence, the jealousy began. It always, always, always start with jealousy.

For the longest time, I could not understand what her problem was with me. I could only speculate that it may have been my eyes.

Under fluorescent lighting, my eyes can change from light brown to light gray to grayish-blue in the blink of an eye.

When Charlotte first gazed into my eyes, her facial expression changed. I got that a lot. I have amazing eyes for a Sista.

Compliments to my mother, and her father. Plus, my boobs and legs were to die for.

CHAPTER 3

Joni and I were like Siamese twins, connected by love. I was three years older than Joni was, and I hated leaving her behind when I went off to Stanford University. I also thought I had escaped the dramas of high school.

As it turned out, this college was no better than high school. It was just a different level of mean girls and childish boys. But I had grown into a voluptuous goddess, like my mother, and paid little to no mind to envy or moronic controversy.

Charlotte, her prestige, her money, and her minions tailgated me to Stanford. If I had known that narcissistic little bitch was going to Stanford, I would have attended Brown or Berkeley.

Charlotte was an arrogant, self-aggrandizing, pompous, malicious, messy little twit. She stole my rich boyfriend, and my poor one, and had turned other college students against me.

Whatever Charlotte could think of to make my life a living hell, she did not hesitate to do. That covetous bitch!

I was not her only target, a couple of guys from my classes were also on Charlotte's hit list, Ronald and Marty, or as she called them, "The Fairies of Stanford."

One day as I was coming from study hall, Ronald and Marty were passing Charlotte and her cronies. Charlotte had made remarks toward Ronald and Marty that enraged me.

They had been trying to keep their gayness a secret until Charlotte outed them. I came to their defense, and we have been besties ever since.

Stanford was an elite university, and confrontations were huge on Stanford's "no, no" list. Charlotte was exempt from those rules.

Her parents had bought her passage into Stanford with monstrous donations. So, the staff would turn a blind eye whenever Charlotte would be Charlotte.

Ronald, Marty, and I would sit around, in my dorm room, for hours on end making fun of Charlotte and plotting revenge. That was our way of getting even with her for each time she embarrassed or insulted us—which was a lot.

I often spoke to Ronald and Marty of the little sister I had left behind, and they were eager to meet her. Knowing Joni and her tenacious holier- than- thou principles *and* Marty being gay and proud of it, I put off Joni's visit for as long as I could.

When I had run out of excuses, I finally arranged for Joni to visit me at Stanford. As I introduced Joni to Ronald and Marty, she immediately did not like them because Joni was against anything or anyone that lived against the Bible, in her view.

The whole time she was there, Marty and Joni had repeated cat-fights. There were shouting matches, hair pulling, eye scratching, and name-calling. With my hindsight, I should have known better than to put those two in the same room.

Anyway, as much fun as college was and making fun of Charlotte was, I needed to concentrate on my future. I decided to start my own business.

After my graduation, I chose to move back home to New Orleans, Louisiana, to open my advertising firm.

Charlotte had moved to Boston. She had landed a job with a reputable company, which was good because of my newly found valor, New Orleans was no longer big enough for both of us.

For my business loan, I chose a particular bank because a Mr. Hot-tie Mack, my loan officer, at that bank drove a Mercedes. He was tall, good-looking, intelligent, and a body that made God himself proud. *Why not?* I thought. We dated for a while and then nothing.

Well, I got a loan and started my business. I gave it my fatherless name: Thompson Advertising Agency LLC.

My mom and Joni came to my grand opening. I think, for the second time in my life, my mother was proud of me. The first time was when I graduated from college and with honors.

My grand opening was where Joni had introduced me to her (although she did not know it yet) husband, Steven. Joni chose well. He was good looking and intelligent.

It was funny how Joni and I both adored smart men. The looks part was optional, but he had to be smart. Joni hit the jackpot—good looks and brains.

Joni soon became Mrs. Steven Dallas, with a darling set of twins— Javon and Lovec. She had become a Christian like our mother, and I had become a semi-black sheep.

I envied Joni. I wanted a two-income family with a few kids attached, but at that time in my life, I loved what I did and could not see myself giving up on my dream.

Okay, enough of that, back to why I wrote this saga.

***

The hooded figure stood in the shadows across the street, lurking-watching. "The little bastard child is starting her own business," the figure pretending to read the newspaper said.

***

CHAPTER 4

My business had soared. I had hired a few associates from my college classes and some locals. Ronald and Marty were my marketing execs.

Ronald was dependable, sensible, and focused. He was a little short and slightly plump. Marty was more of a drama queen; and had the attention span of a five-year-old. He was slightly tall and had a slender build. Both of them were quite handsome.

In college, we had all the same classes and had nightly study and Charlotte sessions. Those S&C sessions sometimes led into the early hours of the morning and a few bottles of Merlot. That is how Ronald and Marty came to be my right hands.

My business was doing fine until I landed the Healthy Pets account. Healthy Pets—was the name of the company that hired my company to launch an extensive campaign. The contract stated that we were to build an internet store and introduce their new product, Rx Pet Chow.

Healthy Pets sales had dropped drastically, and it was up to my staff and me to come up with a clever slogan and marketing strategy to boost those sales.

My team had been baffled for months, and we were nearing our deadline when Ronald and Marty suggested bringing in outside help.

CHAPTER 5

The trees that lined Canal Street had started to show signs of an approaching fall. Leaves were turning brown. Birds had fled for the winter, and caterpillars nestled snuggly in their cocoons awaiting chrysalis.

The ambiance was disquieting that day. The chill in the air emerged ominously. The rain poured with boldness. The clouds were dark gray and eerily rippled. The wind shrieked like a banshee, and the lightening was attacking the city with anger.

It was one of those days when you had that feeling of dread that you could not shake off. No matter how hard you tried to think of something pleasant, that menacing feeling would not go away.

Like something, somewhere was trying to deliver a warning that a storm was coming. It would be a sinister storm, something wicked, something bad.

I looked around the room to see if anyone else was displaying that feeling of doom as I had, but everyone seemed happy as usual. Not one of them looked melancholy.

I sat looking out the window, watching the rainfall drench the city, eagerly anticipating the new hire's arrival. Mr. Marcus Mackenzie.

Mr. Mackenzie was born and raised in Manchester, somewhere in England. He attended college at Boston University and had studied marketing abroad on several continents, learning different cultural desires and needs.

Marcus was one of the leading freelance marketing consultants in Boston. I had never met him, but his reputation did pave the way. We were fortunate to get him.

Ronald and Marty had talked me into hiring him. They even flew to Boston to interview him. The rave reviews, the "he is the best," the "his skills are impeccable," and the "he is to die for hot" convinced me to bring him on board.

His salary demands were befitting his proficiency, but I could have hired someone fresh out of college who was hungry to make a name for him or herself for a lot less.

I hired him on a trial basis. I gave him one year to show me what he can do. Plus, I thought it would be nice to have someone around the office that I could engage in adult conversations.

Besides, we did need help with the Healthy Pets account. Ronald and Marty said he was so good, that he could convince President Obama to buy the Brooklyn Bridge.

CHAPTER 6

My staff was in the conference room, waiting to eye the new arrival. Ronald and Marty had told everyone how *caliente* (hot) he was. His physical appearance did not matter to me. Until I saw him.

I was looking at the clock on the wall and noticed it was now nine-twenty. The new guy was scheduled to arrive at nine sharp. I did not bitch too much about the time because of the horrid rain dance that was going on outside.

Still, with the money I was paying him, I would have thought he would have made an extra effort to be at work on time.

Ronald and Marty were prancing around the office like nervous little scaredy-cats, in fear of my wrath. They were on the receiving end of one of my intimidating stares just as he walked in.

"Damn!" I said, removing my glasses from my eyes. I thought I had safely spoken those words in my head, only to realize I had said them out aloud by the way everyone turned and looked at me.

I was not the only one; all the women were drooling. Marty leaned close to me and said, "Close your mouth before something flies in it."

I hurriedly shut my mouth, wiping off the drool in the corners. I took a quick look at Marcus to see if he had noticed. Thank God, he had not.

Ronald had begun to introduce Marcus to the staff members, giving me the diversion I needed to recoup. Then it was my turn. I clumsily stood to shake his hand. When he said hello Ms. Thompson, his accent caught me off guard. That sexy British accent.

"I'm Ms...." Nothing came out. Luckily, for me, Ronald stepped in and sarcastically said, "This is Ms. Thompson, the owner of the company, and the one that will be paying your salary."

It was a little unnerving how

protective Ronald and Marty were of me. They were like big brothers that never wanted their little sister to date. Or, they did not think any boy was good enough for me.

Nevertheless, I looked into Marcus's eyes—the eyes being the windows to the soul and all—and saw the Pied Piper, and I was the rat being led to something wonderful.

Ronald gave me a little nudge to bring me back from wherever in the hell I had mentally drifted off. The need to want to give Ronald a ghetto chastising overwhelmed me, but I did not want to exhibit the hood in me in front of Marcus.

I could not believe how I had stumbled on my name so that Ronald had to say it for me. I felt as goofy as the school's nerd asking the hottest girl in school to the prom.

He said, "Nice to meet you, Ms. Thompson." When he spoke my name, my knees nearly gave away. I had to sit down before I embarrassed myself any further.

My heart was racing. My body was hastening to pump out those happy little endorphins. The room was getting hotter by the second, and I was beginning to perspire little beads of lust.

I started to fan with the nearest object I could find. Unfortunately, it was a binder loaded with paperwork. Paper began to fly everywhere.

Marty was sucking his teeth, tsk, tsk, tsk. Ronald shook his head, saying, hm, hm, hm, Ronald, and Marty said, simultaneously, "That is so sad."

Marcus turned to look at me and gave me a comforting, reassuring smile. Thank God I was sitting down. Marcus was truly the embodiment of tall, dark, and handsome—eye candy that you wanted to eat all day long.

After the introductions were over, he took off his dark blue Armani suit coat, revealing his light blue Versace shirt. Oh—My—God! That time I was careful that *those* words had been safely spoken in my head.

The gods had worked in unity, creating that splendor of man. Thank you, Adonis, Eros, Aphrodite, and Apollo.

As Marcus held up his left hand to ask a question, his left finger showed no sign of a wedding band. "Happy birthday to me!" I sang to myself, secretly clapping my hands under the table.

Later, I hadn't realized I had a pen in my mouth, staring at Marcus's chest—imagining what it was like under his shirt—until Marty reached over and jerked the pen out of my mouth.

"Lord, I hope this woman gets some sex soon because she is embarrassing the hell out of all of us," he said as he walked away.

Marty did not realize how close he had come to the receiving end of my backhand. Ronald, the more sensible one, gave me a distant high-five.

I couldn't help but admire that specimen of a man. I knew from the moment I saw him that I wanted to sleep with him. I wanted to feel those muscular arms around me. I wanted to feel those rugged hands all over my body. I wanted to bath in ecstasy with that hunk of RICH, DARK, CHOCOLATE.

CHAPTER 7

After the meeting was over and everyone had returned to their workflow, Ronald and Marty could not wait to come to my office to remind me of the sad display of attraction I had publicized in front of everyone.

"How long has it been since someone took a peek under that skirt, Ms. Thang?" asked Marty.

"I've been busy," I replied.

"Honey, no one is ever too busy for sex. Especially if you enjoy it," said Ronald.

"Wait, what?" asked Marty, looking confused.

"Well, I am. Now get out the hell of my office!" I snapped.

"Don't let this one get away from your snotty ass," Ronald said, grabbing Marty's arm as they walked away.

They both laughed after Marty said, "She knows she got cobwebs growing down there."

I looked down at my "down-there" part and thought to myself, 'I am not snotty. I'm just selective, very selective, and I do not have cobwebs growing down there.'

"Dear God, how long has it been? Lately, I had been very busy with clients that left little time for dating. But in retrospect, I can say I did have a few friends, *ish.*

"There was—uh, what was his name with the Mercedes? He was very good in bed. He could have been a nice suitor, but he was a mammoth snob.

"And, there was that other one who was reasonably romantic. Only that one had mommy and daddy issues—we would have been codependent.

"And, there was the one with the yacht. That one would have been a good catch if he had not looked at himself in the mirror more than I did.

"And there was Mr. Tall. Okay, I do not know what the hell I saw in him. I guess I was just horny and needed to get laid.

"And there was Big Daddy, who wasn't so *big*. I liked him because he was much older than me. I had tried men in my age bracket, but it hadn't worked out.

"So, I thought I would take a dip in the senior-citizen pool. He turned out to be going through male menopause and had mentally reverted to his teen years.

"I did not have the time nor the patience to deal with a grown-ass man trying to relive sixteen again. It was not as if I had not tried.

"I guess I suffer from mommy and daddy issues, bastard child syndrome, or abandonment disorder.

"Whatever the reason, there I was, thirty-five years old, with no husband, no kids, and no one significant in my life. If I do not land a man soon, I might develop cobwebs down there.

CHAPTER 8

Business, as usual, took place around the office. We all busied ourselves with demographics and targets, and segments and geographies while trying to figure out a killer slogan for the Internet campaign.

We were four months into a six-month deadline, and we were still stumped. I needed Mr. Perfect to earn his wages.

A little over a month later, we finally launched the account. Rx Pet Chow had been broadcast on the television, showcased on the Internet, and written about in the Times. Not to mention, Rx Pet Chow was on almost every dog food shelf in America.

The cleverly thought of slogan was by our own, Mr. McKenzie, "Rx Pet Chow, "The perfect recipe for a healthy pet." Why hadn't I thought of that?

Anyway, I was pleased with my team, so I threw an office party. Mr. Flawless did not attend. For some reason, his absence made my heartache. I was crushing on a man I hardly knew. Or, should I say, I was lusting for a man I hardly knew.

In my head, I envisioned our wedding. The kind of house we would live in, with our four children running through the house.

Marcus would be yelling at our kids to simmer down, while sitting on the sofa watching the evening news, with a glass of brandy in his hand.

I would be in the kitchen on the phone with Joni, telling her about my day while making dinner. In my mind's eye.

***

The hooded figure stood across the street in the cold and rain, staring at the occupants moving around inside the office building — remembering.

***

CHAPTER 9

It had been days since Mr. Perfect decorated my space with his presence. Every time I caught a glimpse of him, it made me want him more.

My desire/lust for him had grown so obvious that he would catch me staring at him, and in return, he would give me an engrossing smile.

Maybe that engrossing smile was just in my head. He has got to have a girlfriend, or boyfriend, or something in between. A man like that could not be alone. Maybe he chose to be.

Weeks passed, and Marcus and I played the phone tag game. I would call him, or he would call me, and neither of us would answer the phone, so the other one would have to leave a message.

Well, that is what I did so I could play his messages, again and again, to hear his voice. Every time someone passed my office, I would look up, hoping it was Marcus. Wishing it was Marcus.

On a few occasions, I would walk past him, look into his eyes, give him a slight smile, put my head down, and keep walking. Just to let him know I was interested.

That's an old trick my grandmother taught me. For some reason, that gesture stimulates something in a man. On other occasions, he would give me a sexually intense stare.

I had to admit it had been a while since I had a hankering for a male partner. Seeing this grandeur of a specimen was causing my hormones to go into overload.

I prayed that God would embellish my bed with that gorgeous hunk of dark chocolate. I asked God to let me take just one bite. I did not care how much gym time would be needed afterward.

CHAPTER 10

The following Sunday, I thought I would go to the office to pick up some papers I had left behind.

As I was walking down the hall to my office, I heard a noise. I thought it was the janitor that comes in on Sundays, so I ignored the sound.

When I got to my office, I noticed Marcus' office door at the end of the hall was ajar. Out of curiosity, I peeked my head in a little. It seemed as though Marcus had some catch-up work to do also.

I spoke to him briefly, hurried to my office, and closed the door. I stood with my back behind the door, trying to defuse the whirlwind of emotions that was causing me to have a Marcus panic.

I had been waiting for a chance to be alone with him, and now that the time had come, what did I do, run to my office and close the door.

The vague knocking that I was hearing seemed distant that at first, I paid it no mind until I realized it was right behind me.

I assumed it was the janitor coming to clean my office next. I slowly opened the door and stuck my head out, and it was Marcus. Then it finally happened.

He eased the door open wider, backing me slowly toward my desk, closing and locking the door behind him.

His eyes were gazing into mine. Non-Christian thoughts were running rampant in my head.

"Je te veux," he said.

I did not know what he had said, but it sounded good. He moved in closer to me and hypnotized me with that enchanting stare of his.

Then his lips embraced mine. I closed my eyes and allowed my mind to bath in wonderment. I allowed my body to let go of my inhibitions and enjoy the ecstasy. Little droplets of his sweat began to moisturize my skin.

His tongue penetrated my inviting mouth like the slither of a serpent. He began stroking and massaging my neck with his lips and tongue.

He slowly unbuttoned my blouse, exposing my red laced bra as he leaned down to kiss my breast. He used his other hand to skillfully glide up my thigh, lifting my skirt, revealing my red laced panties.

His hand found its way to my lower erogenous zone. Those warm hands gently caressed it. My body blushed with delightful agony. My inner desires screamed with pleasure.

Although I did enjoy the foreplay, I wanted him to penetrate me. He took both my hands and held them firmly behind my back while he continued to moisturize my neck with his tongue and lips.

I shivered as his lips pressed firmly against my bare skin. I could feel the hardness of his male region against my wanting flesh. I wanted that region inside me.

He released my hands and held me close to him while he continued to knead my breast. I wrapped my arms around his neck while kissing him intensely.

He cupped my breast and began to massage it, causing waves of erotica to rush to my erogenous zones. Currents of wonderful were surging through my skin.

My deepest, most carnal needs unmasked the primal side of me. I moaned and groaned with sexual gratification. My head was spinning incoherently—my mind swam in an ocean of trance.

I was a female volcano about to erupt. Marcus looked at his watch and said, "Shit! I gotta go." It took me a second to shake myself out of Marcus-land. What the fuck just happened!? Did that mother...just walk... off? What the hell?

Loving a Married Man

I was still in the moment. My blouse was doused with lust. My breast was swollen and still tingling from the thrill of his touch. And, my gametes were ready to mate with his gametes.

That bastard left me standing there breathing like a dragon, perspiring like a six-hundred-pound-man, and with my erogenous zones begging for more of his amore.

I was so weak I fell to my knees. I had to hold my legs close together to ease that feeling of refusal. No man had ever...

Again...! "What the fuck!?" What was so important that he had to leave me like that? Who leaves in the middle of sex? Dear God, please control my anger and refrain me from shooting that bastard when I see him again. Damn!

***

An angry and vengefully charged person was plotting retaliation. Time is supposed to heal all wounds and bring closure. Time had not healed that wound. But death would bring some closure.

***

CHAPTER 11

Joni had called wanting to have a sister-time dinner date, but I was not in the mood. I decided to stay in that evening and drown my sorrows with liquid spirits. I was still trying to wrap my head around what had happened earlier.

Besides, my mind would only be on Marcus's remarkable hands, tongue, lips, and whatever were waiting for me in his pants. I couldn't stop thinking of the things we would do to each other.

I had to make love to him. I needed to have him in me, on me, and everywhere in-between. I needed to feel his arms around me again. Is this the way love feels? All this pining and wanting someone so badly until it hurts.

I was so restless. I was tossing and turning. My body was exhausted, but my mind would not let me sleep. Visions of Marcus and me making love grabbed hold of my mind and would not allow me to think of anything else.

I mused over how his tongue traced my neck while I mimicked his actions with my own hands.

I had spent the whole night thinking of the things he did with his body parts to my body parts. Just thinking about it made me clammy.

That blinding morning sun ended my imaginary sex–play with Marcus, and I realized I had not gotten a wink of sleep.

I could barely shower and could not think about holding down breakfast. Even trying to dress for work was hard. I put my underwear on backward. Twice! And I burned my favorite/sexy blouse that I wanted to wear to seduce Marcus.

How could I face him? What would I say to him? How could I see him walk around the office after the way he walked out on me?

I felt as though he had left me standing alone at the altar. I thought about firing his ass, but his contract was for a year, and he still had roughly seven months to go.

Why he stopped had me confused. Maybe there is someone in his life he doesn't want to cheat on. I can respect that. I can't accept the fact that he didn't want me. I'm hot!

Maybe he is like most men?. Maybe he prefers a woman with fewer options. Men see a woman with lots of options as intimidating.

CHAPTER 12

I did not think any of the do-rights at the office knew what had happened yesterday, but I could not help wonder if Marcus had told his boys at the office. Who, in turn, had told their girls at the office. Who, in turn, had told other girls at the office.

What kind of reception would greet me, as I entered my workplace, if they knew? Would I get raw stares, hear jealous whispers, laughter, or even worse, the silent treatment?

I could not think of anything more humiliating than to have those preacher wife wannabes' in my private business.

As I entered my workplace, I quickly traipsed the walk - of - shame to my office and closed the door.

I sat at my desk, still trying to figure out why he pulled back. Contracts, posters, and invoices that needed my signature and attention cluttered my desk, but it all had to wait.

Loving a Married Man

My mind was full of questions that needed answers. While I dealt with these unfamiliar emotions, I had my office phone and cell phone on do- not- disturb mode. The only disturbance I wanted at that moment was, Marcus.

Why didn't he finish me? What was so important that he had to stop? Did he have somewhere else to be? He did look at his watch.

Before you know it, it was nearly lunchtime, and the light on my answering machine was blinking.

I had not planned to leave my office until everyone had gone home, but Joni was one of the callers that had left a message on my machine inviting me to lunch since dinner was a *no*.

CHAPTER 13

Joni chose our favorite restaurant in the French Quarter. This restaurant had a way of blackening redfish that melted in your mouth and left you (even though you were full) wanting more.

She took one look at me and innately knew something wrong. It always amazed our mother at how in sync we were, like genuine twins.

"Ok, spill!" Joni demanded.

"Spill what? I asked modestly.

"Don't do that."

"Don't do what?"

"That cover-up thing that you always try to do. Especially when you are dealing with something emotional. What happened?"

"Alright. I know there's no point in trying to keep anything from you."

"Damn straight. Start talking."

After I told Joni of the incident in my office, she began to laugh hysterically. Not finding it funny, I threw my dinner roll at her.

"I can't believe you don't know what he just did to you?" Joni asked.

Unfortunately, I did not. Joni told me that Marcus had played one of the oldest mind games men play on women called "the sexual-mind game."

"The sexual what?" I asked

"The sexual-mind game. Where he gives you a little bit, just enough to put him heavy on your mind, then he pulls back. Now, you are wondering why he pulled back and what else does he have to offer.

"That will make you want him even more. For days, he will pretend like it never happened and ignore you, which will drive you insane. He knows you want him/it.

"He knows you are thinking about him/it. And, he'll know when you are ripe for the pickings. By then, you will be ready to give it up whenever, wherever he wants it."

"Experience or hearsay?" I asked.

"Experience. And, when you finally get it, and it is good, you fall harder than you have ever fallen and surrender yourself."

I asked Joni how she had handled it. Joni said she never did; it handled her. She still pined for him.

"Don't get me wrong, Joni said. "I love my husband to death, but sometimes when we are making love, I let my mind drift on that other man. I can't believe an educated woman like yourself never heard of the sexual-mind game."

"I can't believe a Christian like you knows of the sexual-mind game. And, I can't believe you were not a virgin when you got married."

"Girl, please! We live in the twenty-first century; nobody is a virgin when they get married," Joni said, reaching over the table and knocking on my forehead.

I pushed her hand away, irately. Joni seemed to know more than me when it came to sex and men. I felt some kind of way, me being the older sister. I am supposed to give her advice on sex and men.

After lunch was over, we hugged, promised to talk more often, and went to our cars. I sat in my car for at least twenty minutes, recalling the office sex-play.

I was getting saturated thinking about it. Jesus! What is wrong with me? I'm starting to feel like a sixteen-year-old virgin that fooled around for the first time.

His touch was so spellbinding. His soft lips on my bare flesh made my hormones do the happy dance. Sexual bliss overcame me when I thought of what was waiting for me in his pants.

The thought caused me to shiver a little. That was a man that knew where all the vital parts of a female were.

When he held me in his arms—those splendid arms—he aroused a whirlwind of emotions that traveled throughout my body like a tornado. I never had, in my life, experienced so much pleasure with a man and never had, in my life, felt such desertion from a man.

It wasn't just that he was fine, good-looking, and smart. Or that he could melt my butter in cold weather. Or, his captivating accent. There was something about *that* man that made my world easier to live in.

Marcus had bewitched me. He had cast his spell, and I was more than willing to fall under his curse.

***

The female unsub was busy planning the scheme for her big day. She was on the phone ordering murder.

***

CHAPTER 14

The following morning, I saw Marcus standing at the water cooler. I decided to pretend the other day had never happened by walking past him as though he were not there. *As Joni said, he would do me.* When I passed him, he leaned over and whispered in my ear, "Bonjour Mademoiselle."

I felt light-headed, and I didn't think my knees would support me for much longer. I felt as if I would fall, so I intended to grab hold of something to keep my balance.

The last thing I wanted was for him to see me fall flat on my ass. To help steady my ground, I grabbed the nearest thing.

Unfortunately, it was a coat rack. Down I went, and the coat rack and coats with me. I felt so humiliated. Not that I had fallen, but that Marcus had seen it.

"Fall arse over tit over, love?" Marcus smirked, reaching for my hand.

Loving a Married Man

I slapped his hand away, picked myself up, and walked away with my head and chest in the air. I couldn't show him my embarrassment.

Of all the people to witness my moment of shame, it had to be Marty. He was giving me that look of disgrace. I wanted to reach out and smack his ass, but the need to hurry to my office and crawl in my imaginary shell took precedence.

I sat in my office and waited nearly an hour for Marty to tell Ronald, after which both of them would come to my office to get their jokes on. Instead, Marcus came.

"Are you all right?" he asked.

"Fine," I replied firmly, with a bit of cynicism, while fiddling with some papers on my desk.

"Okay, boss lady. You know where I am if you need me," he said, walking away with both hands in the air.

'If I...Negro, please!' What I needed was for him to finish what he had started. Oh, God, I *really* needed him to finish what he had started! I did not just need the sex; I needed him. Everything he was, everything he is, and everything he would be.

As he walked off, I could not help but look at how his buns were hugging those Gordie jeans. I wanted to grab a handful and squeeze the stuffing out of them.

Joni was right. I would do him right here on the floor if he wanted.

CHAPTER 15

I could not stress how anxious I had become. I couldn't remember wanting anything so badly, let alone a person. I could not concentrate on work, play, well, maybe play, but nothing else. I needed to be with Marcus.

Seeing Marcus walk around the office and not be able to express my passion for him was killing me. He had a strong and confident stride.

An ass that should be in the Library of Congress—firm and just round enough to be noticed, joined by muscles that should be cloned. And, oh my God, his lips.

The things I imagined doing to Marcus had God himself with one eyebrow raised. I did not know how much longer I would have been able to hold back on that hunger.

I thought about sleeping with my neighbor, who had been after me for years, to feed that hunger. Then I thought, only Marcus had the power to feed that hunger.

I knew, if the chance presented itself, I would do him whenever, wherever he wanted. Damn you, Joni! When did my little sister surpass me in intelligence?

*** Maybe I feel this way because I had never allowed myself to care too much for any man. I did not want to end up like my mother.

My mother never went out on dates. Joni and I were her whole world. I refused to spend my Friday and Saturday nights like my mother listening to the fun Joni and I had.

I often pondered what had happened to my mother. Was it a man that had hurt her so deeply that she'd given up on love? Who had shattered her world, or had betrayed her? Was it my father? Did he leave her standing alone at the altar?

I vaguely remember a man when I was very young. After that, I never saw my mother with another man. I sometimes wondered who he was and where is he now.? Was he our father? What made him leave us? What made him leave our mother?

She would sit at the window for the longest time as if she were waiting for someone. Was that it, he said he would return and never did?

Other times, she seemed to be in nowhere land. Most nights, Joni and I could hear her crying in her room when she thought we were asleep. ***

Later that night, I was sitting on the sofa, finishing some office work that I had taken home. As I stood to pour myself another glass of wine, the doorbell rang.

I began to breathe heavily, and my knees locked together; the palms of my hands began to sweat. I wanted it to be Marcus. I wanted a continuance of the other day. Only this time, I wanted him to hit a home run.

But it was Ronald and Marty. Part of me thanked God, and the other part of me felt disappointed that it was not Marcus.

"Why you got that disappointed look on your face? You expecting someone else?" asked Marty as he walked in.

"What if I was?" I said, giving Marty a goofy look. "Hi, Ronald."

"Hey, sweetness, you ready to go?" asked Ronald.

I had forgotten we had made plans to go bowling that night. I was in no condition to hold the bowling ball, let alone bowl. I asked if we could stay in and get white boy wasted.

I wanted to tell them all about my tryst with Marcus, but I could not bring myself to share that humiliating moment, especially not with Marty. I did not need to hear one of his puns that night. Plus, Marty would never let me hear the end of it.

Loving a Married Man

After they had gone, I decided to get some laundry done. I knew I would have another sleepless night.

CHAPTER 16

I had finished my laundry and had returned to my apartment when I could see someone in the corner of my eye as I was about to put the key in the lock on my door. Before I could turn completely, Marcus was in my three-foot space.

The scent of his Versace cologne filled the air. The aroma was sending me into a trance. I was at the mercy of this male divinity.

Je voulais faire cela depuis le premier jour que je t'ai rencontré. Je veux faire l'amour pour (*je t'ai*). God, I loved his French words.

He placed one hand behind my neck, and I dropped the basket on the hall floor. I leaned my head back, inviting him to venture wherever he saw fit. He backed me against the wall, kissing me hungrily.

He massaged my neck with his thumb. As I surrendered, myself to him, I humbly moaned. Joni was right again. He took my keys from my hand and unlocked my door. Then he lifted me with one arm.

I wrapped my legs around him like a fly caught in a Venus flytrap. We entered my apartment, with my legs still wrapped around him, slowly stripping each other of our clothes.

I glanced at my lingerie spread out on the corridor floor and pointed at my clothes as he was closing the door. I think I whispered, "My clothes." I know I said, "To hell with them. If someone steals them, I will buy more."

His soft lips sent thrills up my spine. His kiss was like sweet venom scattering through my veins. Then he said, "Je voulais *tu* dès l'instant où que je t'ai vu."

That kind of talk aroused me to a whole new level. His hand slid up my thighs, slowly moving across my waistline, gently massaging my back and shoulder, rubbing the base of my neckline.

I began to moan loudly. I wanted Marcus to penetrate me and forget the foreplay. My body was aching for him to enter me.

I wanted to feel his manhood inside my womanhood. I needed him to calm that tempest of fire that had been intensifying inside me.

I trembled with delight when his tongue touched my bare skin. I tilted my head side-ward so his thumb could continue to manipulate my neck.

He pressed his male hardness against me as his hand moved slowly up my back. He backed me against the wall and began to suck on my neck passionately. Little beads of desire seeped through the pores of my skin.

His finger traced the mid-line of my breast as he stared into my eyes. One of my hands found his thigh and clutched it, pulling him closer to me. I moisturized my lips in anticipation. Then I thought if this bastard walks away this time, I may have to shoot him.

Loving a Married Man

Finally, the moment I had longed for. Marcus carried me to my bed. He laid me down and penetrated me slowly. He slid in me with the dexterity of a god. As he slid in and out of me, my body sashayed in harmony with the rhythm of his strokes.

The deeper he probed, the more my body squirmed with pleasure. As our bodies clung closer together, his strides became forceful and piercing.

The warmth of my walls persuaded him to thrust faster. His hands embraced my breast while his tongue and lips fondled my neck. My body moaned with rapture at our mutual touch.

With each stroke of his male marvel, my hands gripped his back more tightly. As he arched his back to deepen his prod, I ran my hands across his chest, feeling his rapid heartbeat.

I gripped his head and back while wrapping my legs around him more tightly, lifting my body to meet his last strokes.

My bed danced in concord as we were in melody with each other. In my head, muttered drums were beating softly, slowly in the distance.

As the drums began to beat faster and louder, so did his thrusts, and my body met his every move. The warmth of his breath brushed against my chest as his tongue and lips bathed my breast.

The drums began to beat more rapidly, and so did his force. The room began to spin faster and faster. His breathing became intense. His grip tightened. His moans grew louder. Then he cried out.

As the beating drums began to mellow and fade away, his body shivered as he released his little soldiers into my fortress.

Hearing him moan with that kind of satisfaction gave me a feeling of atonement. Then the mating was complete.

We laid there, touching, kissing, and feeling each other. I could feel Marcus' little soldiers swimming inside of me. My body had never known that kind of pleasure.

CHAPTER 17

After our first sexual encounter, we had our first argument. A girlfriend of mine from my childhood had been trying to reach me because she needed to talk.

She had ended her relationship with her live-in boyfriend of a few years. I called her immediately while Marcus was getting dressed.

I was listening to her but watching him. His body was a work of art, a masterpiece. I just wanted to grab him and lock him away to be at my disposal whenever I needed him.

He overheard the conversation and put in his worthless two cents. My girlfriend had been living with this man for some time and never once asked for anything. The one time she needed money from him, he said he could not help her.

She said she could understand if he could not help her, but she felt he did not want to help her. I had told her years ago when a man starts saying you pay half, and I'll pay half; you are just a roommate with benefits.

Marcus said maybe he thought she was not good enough to receive his money. Hence, a roommate with benefits.

That remark angered me the fuck up. My friend was good enough to sleep with all those years, but she was not good enough to give money to when she needed it.

"That's how some men feel, Cherie," said Marcus. Money is precious to a man, and he has to feel a woman is worth it to get it, and if she is not…tant pis.

"Precious, huh? Well, let me give you and your boys a little food for thought! A woman feels the same way about her body as you men feel about your money!"

Pretending he did not understand what I was saying, he asked, "What?" So, a Sista broke it down for him.

"Let's say you have been giving a woman your precious money each time she asked for it, and whenever you wanted to have sex with her, she would say no. Wouldn't you feel like she was using you?"

"Hell, yeah!" he said.

"It is the same way for a woman. If she is constantly giving her most precious gift to a man, and he will not give her money, when she asks for it, she feels like she is being used.

We, women, have something worth more than gold, we don't have to be no man's fool. Always remember Marcus, what one man won't do, another man will. Got it now, Marcus?"

Marcus said, "Now you've gone all barmy and worked yourself into a state, love." He kissed me on my forehead and walked out of the door.

"Bloody idiot!"

I had worked myself into a mild frenzy. I wanted to call my friend's *roommate* and say a few select words to him that he would never forget. Instead, I called her back and told her to go to the Western Union in the morning.

CHAPTER 18

Still pissed at that night's argument, I did not want to run into Marcus. I had managed to elude him for a few days. I could not believe he and other men could think so little of women.

The anger in me had risen even higher when I saw Marcus talking to Monique, one of my female employees. I wondered if he had slept with her and what he said to her when she asked him for money.

When he saw me, he walked toward me. I still could not have a conversation with him, business or otherwise. I kept thinking, what if that had been me? What would he have said to me?

There was no avoiding him this time; he was coming toward me, and there was nowhere to go but straight ahead. "About the other night, Chérie," he began the conversation. I understood what you were saying, but some men do not think that way, babe.

"No, Marcus, men don't think at all. You men are selfish. You take and take and give little, if anything at all."

"Can we go into your office and discuss this? Or my office, if you prefer," he said, guiding me towards his office.

I had not seen his office in a while. I was quite impressed by the way he decorated it. The man likes the color purple.

His office was overflowing with an assortment of purple things. Purple blinds at the window and purple flowers ranging from light to dark purple.

He also had expensive paintings on the wall. I especially admired the artworks by DaVinci, *The Last Supper*, *Saint John the Baptist,* and *The Virgin and Child with Saint Anne.*

I wondered if they were authentic. The icing on the cake was a huge picture of himself that covered one-third of the 105x130 wall.

"Seriously, dude!"

He was undoubtedly exhibiting the cocky side of himself. His desk was semicircular and clear. That was nice.

He began the conversation by saying he would give me anything I wanted whenever I asked. Part of me believed him, and part of me thought he was saying that to get into my pants again.

If only he knew how much I wanted to give it up—right there on his clear desk—under all his purple stuff and paintings—in front of Jesus and his disciples.

After we had talked for a few minutes, we both agreed never to argue about someone else's situation again.

"Can a brother get some love?" he asked.

'You can get a lot more than just love,' I thought.

He cloaked those virile arms around my waist, looked into my eyes, and said, "I promise to do all I can to keep a smile on your face, Chérie." I wanted to stay right there, suspended in time, in his world.

His exotic winsome cologne was triggering me to clear off his desk, throw him on his desk, and take more of what I had gotten the other night.

Now, I had never considered myself one of those women who lose control or sense of self because she had a nice d**k in her hands, yet there I was, madly in love after only one round.

***

The hooded figure across the street watched with fury as Marcus embraced Vikki. The figure squeezed the hot cup of coffee, spilling it, not caring that the heat from the coffee was burning its hand.

***

CHAPTER 19

Then something happened that caused my trust in Marcus to a nose-dive. On my way home from work one night, I was driving on a desolate road, and I got a flat tire. Even the moon didn't dare venture in that area.

I was so afraid of being on that particular road alone, but it was a shortcut to my apartment building. I was exhausted. I wanted to get home in a hurry, take a shower, and wash the day away.

I was on France Road. It was dark. Even the moon had walked away from that area. The businesses had closed at five or six in the evening, so there was no one around to hear me scream—if I needed to scream.

'Dumb ass, you had to take the short cut,' the angel on my right shoulder shouted. There was always a battle between the angels on my shoulders.

The angel on the right side, the goody-two-shoes, always gnawed in my head about morals and consequences - while the angel on my left side, the rebel, often got me in trouble for doing things immoral and not giving a shit about the consequences.

Anyway, France Road was where certain activities took place, and the NOPD(New Orleans Police Department) BP (Border Patrol) and LP (Levee Police) patrolled to catch criminals in the act. I did not want to be caught in the middle of them catching criminals in the act.

I called roadside assistance, but they could not come for three hours. I called Marcus, and the call went straight to voicemail. So, I sent him a text-still no response.

The one time I needed him, he was not available. That was not keeping a smile on my face. "Why would his phone go straight to voice-mail? I thought. And, where the hell is BORDER PATROL, LEVY POLICE, and NOPD?!

I called Ronald and Marty, and they were there in twenty minutes. They could see it was more than just a flat tire that had me a tad bit upset. The peculiar looks on their faces raised my red flag.

"What's going on in that pretty little pate of yours?" Marty asked.

"Pate, seriously? Someone has been learning his French," I teased.

"We have known you for years, Vikki, we can tell when something is bothering you, and I don't think it's that flat tire," said Ronald.

I told them that I tried to call Marcus before I called them, but his phone went to voicemail.

"Now, why would you call him instead of us?" asked Marty.

Then I told them that I had kinda been seeing Marcus, which is why I had called him first.

"Just say you slept with him," said Marty.

"You, Lil bitch!" I said angrily.

They looked at each other in such a way that I knew they were concealing something from me. Something they needed to tell me but dreaded doing. When I asked, each told the other to tell me.

Marty said, "I told her that the dress she wore out last Saturday night made her look like a drag queen. Your turn!"

Anticipating what Ronald was about to say gave me a very uneasy feeling. The kind of feeling that causes red flags to dance in your head.

Ronald took my hand and said, "Love is a precious gift, and you shouldn't waste it on someone that does not deserve it."

"No need for the preamble, Ronald. Just say it," I demanded, bracing myself for whatever was coming.

Then Ronald crushed my heart so badly he could have made tomato soup out of it. Ronald told me that Marcus was married. I did not want to hear that the man I thought was a keeper wasn't mine to keep.

It felt like I had been hit in the heart with a wrecking ball. I had to lean against my car to keep from falling.

All that time. All the flirting and Marcus never bothered to tell me he was married, even after we had sex! He didn't say a word.

The earth seemed to be collapsing under me, and I was falling into a black hole. I was in love with a married man.

CHAPTER 20

Ronald and Marty had always been a little overly protective of me. I am sure they had noticed the little flirtatious games Marcus and I had been playing.

Ronald and Marty took it upon themselves to find out a little more about our mysterious Mr. Mackenzie.

Now that I had heard he was married, I had to know for sure. I needed to see his wife. I needed to see the woman he went home to every night.

I needed to see the woman that kept him from spending *that* night at my place. Is she the reason he left so suddenly the day of the sexual tease thing and couldn't finish what he had started?

I decided to follow him home one evening, with hopes of catching a glimpse of his wife. I realized later that following him instead of just asking him if he were married was a bit unwise, but that is what I did.

Marcus turned onto Lake Shore Drive, a subdivision for the rich and famous. The houses in that area were five million and up.

'I don't pay him enough to live in this area,' I thought.

He turned again on Lake Shore Estates, where that famous movie star lived. 'What the hell!' I thought. How the hell could he live in an exclusive neighborhood like this?

Then he turned right into a driveway on Lake Shore Estates. It was a French Colonial style mansion. It was so huge it looked like a small hotel instead of a home.

It had an abundant number of windows. There were two lions at the top of the stairs, and yellow and pink roses lined the walkway that leads to the stairs.

A huge cypress tree was on the right side of the front yard, and the lawn was such a pretty green it felt a little bit like Christmas.

Marcus honked his horn, and two little girls ran outside to greet him, and then the shock of my life emerged. It was my old high school and college foe, Charlotte. That would explain how he could afford this neighborhood.

She was nothing like she used to be. I hardly recognized her. Seeing her like that, after all those years, I must admit, gave me pleasure.

Now I can see why he came to me. That *pretty* bitch that had given me so much hell in high school and college was no longer attractive.

Even the kind of clothes she had on didn't seem like Charlotte. She was wearing an oversized navy-blue blouse with black tights underneath and flats.

Not her usual attire, which consisted of a mini- skirt and a low-cut blouse that exposed her chattels. Charlotte, Charlotte, Charlotte. I slept with your husband. I am almost not mad at your husband for being married to you.

Being granted the opportunity to hurt Charlotte was like the feeling you would get from winning the lottery. She had done so much harm to me in high school and college that karma had become my new best friend.

While hugging Charlotte, Marcus spotted my car at the end of the street. He picked up the smallest little girl and walked his family inside, looking back in the direction of my car.

A few minutes later, he walked outside alone and got back into his car. He headed my way. I sped out of that area like a bat out of hell.

As I approached Paris Avenue, the light turned red, and I had no choice but to stop. He pulled his car in front of my driver's side, halfway blocking my car and other cars as well.

He jumped out of his car and rushed toward mine. Subconsciously I wanted to run over his ass. Well, maybe not subconsciously.

I quickly rolled up my windows and locked my doors. I could not possibly talk to Marcus then. Mostly because I did not know what to say.

The cars behind me were honking their horns angrily. Marcus was waving his hands in a simmer-down fashion to the other cars. When he approached my car, he tried to open the door. Realizing it was locked, he said, "Open the door belle."

I kept my eyes on the light waiting for it to turn green so I could drive off. "Come on, babe, let me explain," he pleaded.

Then the light turned green, and I swerved around his car, driving my car on the neutral ground and drove off.

I was pretty sure whatever he was going to say to me would have been a lie, and I was not in the right state of mind to hear one of his lies.

I could see him in my rear-view mirror, just standing there with his shoulders hunched, and his arms open as if waiting to embrace me, ignoring the honking horns.

I knew that I would have to face him tomorrow, but by then, I could have

come up with an acceptable lie as to why
I followed him.

CHAPTER 21

I had not realized that Marcus had familiarized himself with New Orleans enough to have learned a shortcut to my condominium.

When I reached my apartment building, there he was, leaning on his car with his arms folded and legs crossed.

He looked so sexy standing there. Any man in a shirt, tie, and jeans, and with that kind of body, arouses something to me. I wanted to *do* him right there in the streets.

Still, I needed to think of a good enough lie to tell him, because the truth would be too embarrassing for me to admit. Unfortunately, I cannot think up lies that quickly.

So, I decided to take an alternate route and focus solely on his marriage and him not telling me.

I got out of my car, slammed the door, and practically sprinted toward him. We got into a shoving and shouting match. Although, I was the only one shoving and shouting.

"You son of a bitch! Why didn't you tell me you were married?"

"Calmez-*toi*, et laissez moi vous expliquer," he said.

"Speak English!" I snapped.

"Calm down and let me explain," he pleaded.

"Explain what? You can't explain away the fact that you are married."

Marcus did what all men did in a situation like this. He pleaded. He began by explaining his attraction towards me and asked, "Would you have slept with me if you knew I was married?"

"Hell, no!"

"C'est pourquoi b je ne vous ai pas dit tout de suite.*toi* dit pas."

"English, you bastard!"

"That is why I didn't tell you straight away."

"How could you keep something like that from me, Marcus?!"

"Cherie, he said, moving closer to me, I was going to tell you when the time was right."

"When was that going to be? After we had slept together for the thousandth time?"

"We're going to sleep together that many times?!"

"Not now, Marcus!" I said while holding up my index finger and walking away a bit. I felt the need to put some space between us before I smacked the hell out of him. And, he might have hit me back.

"Cherie, I fell la tête sur la colline the moment I met you."

"What?" I don't know what he said, but it seemed like something I would want to hear.

"I fell head over hills for you."

"Wow!" I did like it.

"If it's any consolation, I never loved my wife."

"Well, you must have never loved her at least twice, you made two children with her."

Okay, I know that sounded stupid, but sometimes when you are angry or hurt or both, stupid shit comes out of your mouth.

"She's not happy; I'm not happy."

"Marcus, a woman, can sense when a man does not love her, and it makes her very unhappy. Charlotte did not seem all that unhappy when I saw her."

"For the longest time, I have been putting on a good face for my girls. But, when I met you, I decided to do something I should have done a long time ago, file for a decree absolute ."

"What the hell is that?'

"A divorce." But I couldn't leave my girls with Charlotte. You do not know her temper. I love my girls, and I can't leave them. Not yet."

"I am not falling for that, wait til my kids get old enough to understand, shit."

"I am not asking you to fall for anything. It's the truth. All I am asking is that you trust me and be patient?"

"Trust! You expect me to trust you. You want me to be patient! Nigga, please!

"I only married her because she got pregnant."

"She did not get pregnant by herself. You got her pregnant!"

"I was intoxicated the night we slept together. About a month later, she told me she was pregnant. I didn't purposely get her pregnant. I did what I thought was the right thing to do. So I married her, but I want *you*," he said, hunching his shoulders.

"Did you stop to think of how much this would hurt me when I found out?"

"No."

"Plonker."

Loving a Married Man

When he started telling me things about his wife that put the final straws on the camel's back, I started to feel like he was trying to play me. I could not believe Marcus tried the "mercy fuck" thing with me.

You know when a man tells you all kinds of bad things about his wife so you will feel sorry for him and fuck him out of pity.

Or, he tells you those things so he can get *you* to do the things his wife won't do. Knowing you will do those things because you'll think those things will get him to want you more than her.

Bullshit!

Or, the ever-famous lie that even I tried to convince myself with because I wanted him so badly., "If he wanted her, he wouldn't be here with me." Seriously chick, men are greedy.

And, what woman wouldn't want to hear, "If only I had met you before I met my wife?" Does any of this sound familiar ladies?

I did not fall for any that sympathy shit! MEN SELDOM LEAVE THEIR WIVES! They want something on the side to play with. I knew that I would only be his sidepiece, and that was all I would ever be until he found himself another sidepiece.

But I had already given it up. So, what was Marcus's purpose? His face displayed so much sexual hunger that I so desperately wanted to feed him.

He moved closer to me, held me in his arms, and whispered, "You're adorable, you know that. I had to have you, ma Chérie. Your cute clumsiness made me want you even more. I'm sorry I did not tell you I was married."

"Are you sorry you did not tell me or sorry I found out."

"Both Chérie. I do not want to lose you, and I did not want you to find out this way."

Now, I knew better than to believe any of that malarkey, but I must admit, hearing him say it did make me feel all warm inside. Besides, no man had ever touched my G, H, and I spot the way Marcus had.

I could not give him up, not yet. I knew the day would come that I would have to. I knew I would be the sidepiece in this threesome but, it was worth it to get back at Charlotte, even if it had to be a secret.

For every time she had insulted me, every lark she ever played on me, every lie she ever told on me, Charlotte was finally going to reap what she had sown, secretly.

CHAPTER 22

Houston's was the most exclusive restaurant in New Orleans. The cuisine was like no other place in the world. For that reason, most of the crème de la crème frequented the place.

Marcus had taken me there on a few occasions, and I had often wondered why the waiter's stared at us so much. I just thought it was because we were such a handsome couple.

He was truly tall, dark, and handsome. I stood five feet eight and weighed one hundred forty-five pounds. Dark and Lovely colored auburn *ish* hair—olive-brown skin, not to mention my stand–at–attention–rack.

It was my birthday, and Joni had made plans to take me to Houston's for dinner. It was to be her, her husband, Marcus, and me.

Marcus said he could not make it because he had to return home for a death in his family; he said that he would make it up to me when he returned.

Loving a Married Man

Joni's husband did not want to be the only man. It ended up just being Joni and me. I knew he didn't want to be the only man and have to listen to a couple of cackling hens, as he called us.

Joni did not question or condemn Marcus for not being there for my birthday. Well, not openly, that is. And, she only judged me a little for dating a married man.

Even though she said, she would never date a married man. Dating a married man means you are number two, three, four, or even five, but never number one.

Joni said she could never be so desperate to have a man in her life that she would purposely be second to any woman.

That statement cut like a fucking knife, but I could not tell her how much she had hurt my feelings and my pride. I know she did not mean it. Besides, I wanted to enjoy my day and the exquisite food at Houston's.

Joni had made reservations for a window seat because she knew I liked looking outside.

As we sat at our table, I thought I'd caught a glimpse of someone that favored Marcus walking in the parking lot.

Thinking it could not be him because he was out of town, I ignored the picture in my head.

Several waiters began to whisper, looking in the direction of Joni and me. One of the waiters said to another waiter, peculiarly, "Oh, shit, it's about to go down!" I realized later what that waiter meant.

After a splendid dinner, we ordered dessert. I excused myself and headed for the restroom to reapply. Well, to pee.

I did not know Charlotte and Marcus were also having dinner there. They had finished their meal and were about to leave when a waiter dropped a plate.

I turned in reaction to the noise and saw them. Had it not been for the waiter dropping that plate, they would have made a clean getaway.

Marcus was standing next to Charlotte, with his mouth opened so wide you could fit an Ocean Liner in it. The moment was so awkward that it seemed surreal.

My first thought was, why would he bring Charlotte to the very place he knew I would be celebrating my birthday? Then I remembered I had not told him we were going to Houston's.

And I forgot Charlotte's birthday was on the same day as mine. Still, that bold asshole takes his wife to the same restaurant he brings me to. I know vengeance is for the Lord, so I asked God to turn his head. I got this one!

"Well, hello, Mr. McKenzie," I said sarcastically. If Charlotte did not notice the implication behind that 'hello,' that bitch was dumber than I thought.

"Vikki?" Charlotte asked.

"Hello, Ms. Thompson, Marcus *professionally* addressed me. I would like you to meet my wife."

I was so angry that he lied about being out of town on such an important day for me that instead of saying hello to Charlotte, I blurted out, "Why would I want to meet your wife whether you like it or not?"

Okay, I know that sounded a bit stupid and simple, but he could have been honest with me. He could have told me the truth about why he could not be with me on my birthday.

"How do you know my husband?" Charlotte asked.

I could have said, I am the other woman—which would have given me immense pleasure—but the moment was awkward enough. As mad as I was at him, I could see Marcus was nervous, not knowing what I would say to Charlotte.

"I am his boss," I said.

"You work for her!?" asked Charlotte.

"You know her?" asked Marcus.

"Yes, he does, and yes, she does." Charlotte is my old college foe," I said in a superior tone. And in my head, I said, *'Guess what bitch, I'm fucking your husband!'*

"Foe?" asked Marcus.

"Yes, Marcus, foe, as in archenemy, rival, adversary!" I answered.

"I know what *foe* means, Ms. Thompson. I didn't know you two knew each other."

"Now you do," I said as I walked off. I was a little hurt, but I'd gotten a smidgen of revenge. If Marcus wanted to keep his marriage after that, he was going to have to do some serious damage control.

I could not contain my joy for the look on Charlotte's face when she realized I knew her husband. It was priceless. She looked like a deer caught in headlights.

CHAPTER 23

The next night, Marcus called to apologize. He said he wanted to make it up to me for missing my birthday.

I wanted to tell him to shove his apology so far up his ass, it would take a team of specialists to find it, and then I'd hang up the phone. But there was that part of me that wanted to forgive him.

"Uptown Jams," was playing on the radio as I was getting dressed. I wanted to be sexy, but not slutty. Classy, but not plain. Conservative, but not prudish.

I chose my backless, black-and-silver, wrap-around dress. It was tight enough to show off my figure, but not constricting. Low cut in the front, revealing just enough of my upper assets to be noticed.

My black-and-silver stiletto heels complemented the dress. I wore my three-piece black and silver Ross-Simmons, mother of pearl earrings and necklace set, and my black and silver Ross-Simmons, mother of pearl bracelet.

To add to the elegance and seductiveness, I slipped on black fishnet pantyhose—topped off by a dash of In style's 'Happy' cologne.

My hair was slightly French twisted with the front overlapping my face and little pearl bobby pins, lined neatly, for support.

I grabbed my wine and went into the bathroom to check my makeup. Behind my bathroom door was a full-length mirror. The lighting was better, and I could make sure everything was in place. *Damn near perfect,* I thought.

I set my wine glass down and was headed back into my bedroom to get my purse so I could move it closer to the door. All of a sudden, I froze and could not move.

Through the corner of my eye, I could see the silhouette of someone standing in my bedroom doorway. It sent a chill down my spine.

I quickly turned, knocking the glass of wine in the sink, spilling it on the floor and walls, but no one was there. I glanced into my bedroom. I did not see a soul. I thought I saw my bedroom curtain move a little.

I walked leisurely toward the curtain. I didn't understand why, but the feeling that danger was lurking behind the curtain, scared the shit out of me.

I slowly reached for the curtain while praying that no one was on the other side. Then the doorbell rang, and that sent another chill down my spine. I jumped back so fast I fell on my bed.

I quickly gathered myself and towel- blotted up the wine. I threw the towel in the hamper and headed for the door. Damn! Had the wine taken effect on me that soon? Was I so tired that the wine had me hallucinating?

I walked to the door, holding my chest with my hand as though my heart was going to fall out of its sockets. I saw Marcus, and all that fear melted away.

Especially when I saw the assortment of looks he was giving me: lust, admiration, desire, but most of all, approval.

CHAPTER 24

Marcus took me to a nightclub that he had heard of, near the Lakefront, that overlooked Lake Pontchartrain.

The lights shimmering on the water, the soft music playing, and my date made the atmosphere more romantic, more alluring, more...just more.

Taking place at the club was a tribute for a fallen NOPD officer. His wife was part owner of the club. The turnout was amazing.

Each mourner had candles and disposable sky lanterns. They released the lanterns into the atmosphere later that night. I couldn't help but notice the sadness upon each of their faces. The officer was loved and respected.

They all had on T-shirts with a picture of the police officer on the front and a poem on the back. A few of the mourners made a speech of how much they would miss him.

***It made me think of how much I would miss Marcus if he died or just went away. I wondered if my mother had missed my father because he had died or had just gone away.

Had my mother dated a married man? Did she have two children for him? Did she think he would leave his wife for her?

Maybe that was why she was so depressed all the time. Maybe that was why she never talked about my father. Maybe that was why she never dated anyone else. Maybe he was the love of her life. Maybe?

I excused myself and headed to the ladies' room. When I got back, the band was playing "A Million to One." Marcus reached for my hand and escorted me to the dance floor.

As we slow danced, he gripped my waist as if he were afraid of letting me go. In my head, I was saying, *never let me go.*

Being near Marcus and having him in my world was more than I felt I deserved. Still, he was not mine to deserve. At that moment, I hated Charlotte more than I had ever hated anyone or anything in my life.

Charlotte had the man that should have been mine. When the time came, and I would have to release him, and I knew that time would come, would I be able to? How could I give up my everything?

Could I? When he had filled that *something* in my life. How could I go back to that emptiness? But tonight, just tonight, I pretended Charlotte did not exist. He was all mine.

It made me think of all the things I was going to do to him when I got him back to my apartment. I was going to make that man always remember me.

My thoughts were on doing an exotic dance for him when I got him back to my apartment. As I laid my head on his chest and looked toward our table, I noticed something odd.

Someone was standing near our table-watching us. Even though it was too dark to make out whether it was a male or female, there was something about that person that was familiar. Eerily familiar. I did not know why, at the time, it felt it eerie, but it did.

After we danced and returned to our seats, I looked around for the person, but that person was no longer in the club. I took a sip of my wine, and almost immediately, I began to feel woozy.

My eyelids were getting heavy. The room had started to spin. I was getting sleepy and needed to get home. I figured it was the stress of the day wearing off. That was all I remembered of that evening.

CHAPTER 25

It was one of those dark, stormy nights, which was typical for New Orleans. The lightning patterned the sky. The only sounds you could hear were volatile rainfall and ear-bursting thunder.

I was awakened in the middle of the night by the sound of an explosion. It was so dark I could not see my own hands. I assumed lightning had hit a power line, causing a blackout on my street.

I was feeling exhausted and had a huge, thrashing headache. Like I had been drinking all night. I recalled having two martinis. Anything after that was a blur. Maybe I'd had one too many martinis.

One martini and you're nice and mellow. The second martini is a warning that you should not have a third because you begin to lose your ethics—on everything. If you are foolish enough to have a third martini, someone will be picking your drunk ass up off the floor. Maybe I'd had a third.

I opened my curtains to let some moonlight in, but it was just as dark outside as it was inside my apartment. It was like the moon had taken the night off.

I searched clumsily in the darkness for my cell phone. I was going to use the flashlight on my phone so that I could light a few candles. But then, I heard a noise that seemed to be coming from the kitchen.

Thinking it was Marcus, I went straight to the bathroom. I needed to get a couple of aspirins. I couldn't understand why my head was throbbing so much. I drank all the time and never got a hangover.

After I took the aspirins, I wanted to know how I got home. I went into the kitchen looking for Marcus, but he was nowhere in my apartment.

Maybe, the noise I had heard came from next door, I thought. I crawled back into my bed to nurse my headache and ride out the and the darkness.

Then, I got that eerie feeling again that someone was watching me, standing in the shadows. That feeling of alarm enveloped me. I could sense someone in the room. Waiting and prowling.

The lightning gave just enough light for me to glance through the corner of my eye at a figure that appeared to be standing at the foot of my bed. I closed my eyes, trying to wish it away. Silly, I know.

When I opened my eyes, the figure was gone. My eyes searched wildly around my room, but no one was there. I used the flashlight on my cell phone to search again. Still not a soul.

Had I imagined someone there? Or had that person exited my bedroom and gone to some other room in my condo? I needed to be sure.

I grabbed my Glock and a candle, knocking over a picture of Joni and me, and nervously searched every room. No one was there. No one was in my apartment. Still, I could not shake that feeling of being watched. It gave me the chills.

I was feeling sick, and my headache had gotten worse. I went into my bathroom, with my Glock and candle, to get two more aspirins out of the medicine cabinet.

I sat my Glock on the bathroom sink and opened the bottle of aspirins. I tapped a couple of aspirins in my hand. When I closed the cabinet door to turn on the water, I saw the shadow of a person pass.

Fear stricken, I turned quickly, spilling the aspirins in the sink and on the bathroom floor. I grabbed my Glock, and shakily pointed it at the door. I do not know how long I stood there before I was able to move or speak.

"Who's there?" I stupidly asked. Like he or she was going to answer, "It's me. Your intruder." The light from the candle and lightning gave me enough light to see if anyone was in my bedroom. Empty.

I went into my bedroom, grabbed my cell phone, and quickly dialed 911, then just as quickly I hung up the phone. I had been drinking. My head was aching and spinning.

The last thing I needed was for the NOPD or Levy Police to think I was paranoid. They had more important matters to attend to and did not have time for my imaginary intruder and me.

I went from room to room with the candle and Glock. No one was in my apartment. With the alcohol I had consumed earlier, coupled by my head feeling that way, tripled by the weather, it was no wonder that I had imagined seeing someone.

Besides, this was a secure building. No one was getting passed, Jason. Jason was the doorman, slash-handyman, slash-security.

He was a huge, scary-looking creature like he had done serious time in Sing, Sing, or some other horrible prison. But underneath, he was the sweetest person you could know and was as gentle as a lamb.

CHAPTER 26

Later that morning, Marcus called and asked me to take a ride with him later that evening. *I* was curious to know how I got home.

He said I was so pisse ivre and that he had to carry me home and put me to bed. I asked Marcus what pisse ivre meant? Essentially, it meant drunk. I was so loving that man.

He surprised me with a mini holiday, as he called it. It was a weekend get-a-way to Biloxi, Mississippi, as I called it. He must have heard me speak of the place I loved most in the world and decided to take me there.

We stayed at the Palace Casino Resort, overlooking the beach. The weather had changed, causing the bluish-green water to pound on the rocks with ferocity. Wicked me, I found that arousing.

We arrived in Biloxi a little after five that evening. Marcus suggested I go shopping while he unpacked and made a few business calls. I went on a shopping spree. It was Biloxi, after all.

While I was shopping, I kept getting that feeling of being followed. I could not shake that feeling no matter how hard I tried. I was getting paranoid like that time in college when I had smoked marijuana for the first time. Never did that again.

Even concentrating on thoughts of what I was going to do to Marcus or buying things I did not need, did not help. I kept looking over my shoulder, but no one seemed to be following me.

When I returned to the hotel room, night had fallen. There was a note on the door telling me to, *"Go to the dining area and pour yourself a glass of champagne. Then read the note on the table and follow the flower petals."*

I opened the door. The scent of Jasmine (another of my favorite colognes) filled the air, and soft music was playing. There was a vase with long-stemmed blue tulips (my favorite flower) on the table. How did he know the blue tulip was my favorite flower?

A gold ice bucket with a bottle of Cristal champagne was in the center of the table, along with a champagne glass.

There was another note on the table, and it read, *"Look on the bed and put it on."* I poured myself a glass of champagne. I saw that the blue tulips were shaped into little arrows. I followed the arrows to the bed, treading carefully as not to disturb the petals.

On the bed was a black bikini and sheer black bikini skirt wrap with a note on top of it. That note read, *"Put it on and join me on the beach next to the large rocks."*

I put on the bikini and skirt wrap and headed for the large rocks. With my glass of Cristal in my hand, I walked curiously toward the large boulders.

When I reached the area surrounded by large rocks, I noticed a blanket with candles, another bottle of

Cristal champagne, oldies-but-goodies music playing on a CD player, and a bowl of strawberries. I looked around for Marcus, but he was nowhere in sight.

Just then, Marcus materialized from behind the rocks, holding one long-stemmed blue tulip. In his bare feet he walked toward me. He had on white pants and a white, unbuttoned shirt, exposing his marvelous chest.

He broke the stem, placed the tulip gently behind my ear, and kissed my forehead. As we sat, he topped off my glass and fed me a strawberry.

Then we went for a late-night swim. Even though it was dark, I watched as that marvel of a man swam with confidence in the ocean as he walked with as much confidence on land.

After we fooled around a little in the ocean, causing all the fish to stop and look, Marcus carried me back to the blanked. He gently laid me on the blanket and began kissing me slowly-avidly. My lips parted to embrace the invasion, while his hand strolled over every part of my body.

One hand gently caressed my cheek as he stared into my eyes. I stretched out my arms, permitting him to do with me as he pleased.

He reached behind my neck and untied my bikini top. Then his tongue erotically stroked my neck, easing its way to my mouth.

My body wormed under his as he sensually squeezed my breast. I was aching to feel him inside me again.

He released my breast and used his hand to reach down and untie my skirt wrap and the sides of my bikini bottom, sliding them from under me.

Those bewitching, erotic drums began to beat slowly, seductively, again. My head began to spin as though I were in a trance.

His tongue slid down my shivering and demanding body until he reached my forbidden (to any other man) zone.

Then he lifted his head, looked into my eyes, and asked, "Shall I continue?"

"Yes, yes, yes, please do," I begged. I grabbed Marcus' head and allowed him to enjoy my womanly treasure. His tongue had my body craving the sensation of an orgasm.

Sweat found its way to the surface of my skin and soaked me with desire. He was navigating my lower erogenous zone with precision. I moaned and groaned with agonizing pleasure.

Suddenly, my body began to tremble uncontrollably. I squeezed Marcus' head tightly between my legs. I had to silence myself by placing my hand over my mouth.

I realized then; I was having a male induced orgasm. A bit prematurely, but I had one. It was with such intense pleasure that my body went into a mild convulsion.

Thirty-six years old, and I'd finally had an orgasm that I did not do to myself. And, it was much better than I did to myself.

After he was sure I was completely satisfied, he pulled away. Marcus climbed on top of me and lifted one of my legs high so he could slide into me with ease. His pace began to quicken as he felt me fidgeting under him.

My body shivered with glee at the mastery of his hands and body movements. I grabbed hold of him. I squeezed and pressed him firmly against my naked flesh.

I could feel him swelling inside me. His tongue moved smoothly down my bare skin and found its way to my breast. With one hand, he kneaded my breast fondly while his tongue engaged in recreation with the other one.

I felt a tingle in my soul as his male hardness glided smoothly in and out of my female softness. I gift wrapped my legs around him snugly.

He slowly and eloquently probed in and out of me, sending me into warps of mania. My body shuddered from his every deed and every caress of his tongue.

The warm sand under the blanket and the friction of our body movements generated more heat, causing us to sweat amply. Beads of Marcus' sweat dripped onto my face and mouth. I could taste his salt—his exquisite salt.

With my legs cloaked around him, he grabbed my thigh, pulling me closer to him—lifting my leg higher. His stride began to accelerate. His breathing escalated. His strokes became more forceful. Those bewitching drums began to beat rapidly. I closed my eyes and let my mind drift.

His grinding energy sent mounds of ecstasy to every part of my hungry, starving flesh. I trembled to every beat of his pounding, succulent endeavors.

As the drums began to mellow, we cried out as our sexual thirsts quenched, and we exhaled. I realized at that moment that letting Marcus go was going to be the hardest thing I had ever done.

Loving a Married Man

It was a clear night. So clear, I could almost see heaven. A warm blanket of southernly breeze, veiled us. The ocean brushed mosaic sounds of violins ashore.

He held me tightly, so close to him that I could feel his heart beating. I opened my eyes and saw the stars looking sadly at me.

I pondered at the mystic wonder of this man. As we lay in each other's arms, naked, and gazing at the stars, pain invaded my heart. Dear God, how can I let go of this magnificent specimen?

CHAPTER 27

After the trip to Biloxi, my conscience burdened me relentlessly. I began to think of Charlotte's feelings and Marcus' innocent children. But, why should I have given a damn about Charlotte's feelings after everything she had done to me in the past?

Still, my Christian morals swayed mostly to the children. I thought of Marcus' innocent little girls being casualties of war. I had no desire to harm them or cause them any pain.

Besides, those two angels on my shoulders were moral wrestling again, and this time the good one was winning. Damn that one!

It was getting to be too much for me bear—all the sleepless nights, sneaking around, the loss of appetite, and constant headaches. The 'can't do this, can't go there,' but the worst thing was being second to another woman. I hear you, Joni.

Loving a Married Man

I want a man I can call mine, go anywhere with, do anything with, introduce him to my family and friends, and not have to be ashamed of what I was doing.

Most of all, even though I did not consider myself a Christian, per se, I felt I was betraying God's words.

My world was falling off its axis, and I was holding on for dear life. I finally fell in love, and it had to be with a married man.

I needed to vent to Joni, even though I knew what she would say, her pretentious attitude gave me second thoughts about confessing my feelings to her.

Still, there was no one else on this earth that I could totally and honestly vent with. When Joni picked up the phone, I could hear my Lil niece and nephew in the background, drowning out the sounds of the television.

"Hey, baby girl, I need to talk."

"Is it about your boy toy?"

"Stop calling him that! He is not my boy toy!"

"My bad, the married man you are having sex with."

"I think I liked *boy-toy* better. Puritanical bitch!"

Just then, I realized my sister had branded me with that shameful, letter, "A." Being married, she had become part of the married women's club.

I could not blame her for the way she was feeling. I know marriage is a sacred vow you make in front of God not to be tampered with by philandering women like myself.

However, when I saw that Charlotte was Marcus' wife, I thought, whoever the god of vengeance was, he was finally on my side.

So, what the hell was wrong with me? Why was that revenge not as vengefully fulfilling as I'd thought it would be?

Then I heard Joni ask, "You know he won't leave his wife, right?" That was not the direction I wanted the conversation to go in. *I just wanted to vent.*

"Who asked him to?" I replied.

"But you do know that, right?" she asked or stated again.

The angel on my left side did want him to leave Charlotte and come running into my arms, but the angel on my right side knew I was only his sidepiece, and if I allowed it to continue, that was all I would ever be.

Hearing, but not listening to what Joni was saying, my mind took a break from her prissy-ass, verbal posture, and I remembered what my aunt Verna had once said when I asked her about men cheating and why her husband did not.

CHAPTER 28

My uncle, Robert, was kind, loving, and attentive to my Aunt Verna. He adored her and did not mind showing it. He never cheated on her, or at least not that I knew. Once, I asked her how she kept him from straying.

Her reply was, "He doesn't stray because he doesn't want to. Most women think if they sex a man right, he will not cheat. The problem with that is there will always be another female whose sex will be better.

"Some think changing themselves for him will work. You should not have to change who you are for anyone. Some think it is their physical appearance. That is just superficial.

"The truth is, there will be something that a man will notice about you that he never noticed in any other woman. You cannot see it, buy it, or make it. It is something about you that will cause him to become instantly smitten.

"It will make his heart skip a beat. Whatever that thing is, your uncle noticed it in me. And that's what keeps him home." *I guess Marcus did not notice that thing in Charlotte.*

My aunt Verna was always so deep! I could have used her advice instead of the shitload of guilt Joni was dishing out.

Oh, who am I kidding! I knew exactly what my aunt would say. "You are sinning heifer—stop it!" Then she and Joni would team up on me. Telling me, I would burn in hell.

Although my Aunt Verna was not as Christianized as my mother, she still had a set of moral values that she respected.

When I decided to let my mind join the conversation with Joni again, she was still going on and on about why he would not leave his wife for me, why I should find a man of my own. You know, all that guilt-ridden shit.

"What is so special about you that would make him abandon his family? If you did get him, do you think he would ever trust you? Would you ever trust him?

"Neither of you would have any trust for the other because in your mind you both would be thinking he or she cheated *with* me—how long would it be before he or she cheats *on* me? Your relationship would be doomed from the start."

Bitch! I wanted to hang up on her judgmental ass, but I knew what she was saying was true. Then she went on and on about why men cheat.

Some men get bored with the same piece of ass. Some men seek compensation through a variety of women (you know, little man part) or because there are so many women and so little time.

Some do it just for the sport. With some, the opportunity happened to present itself. Some are confused. But mostly some are still searching for that one, that will make his heart skip a beat.

Then she said something else that was somewhat true. "What men don't know is women get tired of the same sex, too, but we have a built-in mechanism called menopause.

We naturally lose the desire for sex altogether. So, we don't have to cheat and compromise our marriage or bodies."

That was the Joni I knew and loved. Then she said, "if a woman cheats, there is usually a reason. It's got to be physically, financially, or emotionally — the three triggers.

I could not believe my little sister, the Christian, knew all of that. She did have a point, though. For most women, if she cheats, there is a reason behind the cheating. My favorites are; an eye for an eye or what's good for the gander is good for the goose.

I left the conversation feeling worse than I had before I'd made that call. That winch took me to a whole new plane of guilt.

I kept thinking of how I would feel if it were me, and another woman was sleeping with my husband—if another woman took my husband away from my children.

Marcus had told me he stayed married to Charlotte for the children's sake. I thought it was because Charlotte had so much money. Had he been using and lying to me all this time?

At that point, I knew what I had to do. Ending it with Marcus would stop the moral wrestling between those two angels on my shoulders. Those two little heifers were the reason for my constant headaches.

The guilt I was feeling had me thinking about my mother. What would she say if she ever found out about Marcus and me, when so many times she had warned us against dating married men? It would break her heart.

Not to mention, I would become a full-fledged black sheep again. I didn't think I could stand to see the disappointment in my mother's eyes. Or, to have my mother and Joni preaching at me.

CHAPTER 29

I woke the following Monday feeling mentally and physically sick. It took every ounce of will-power I could muster to get out of bed.

I hopped into the shower, hoping to wash away some of the guilt that had me with those less than desirable feelings.

I was also feeling kind of woozy. I had a few employees out with the flu. So, I drank two large glasses of orange juice and took some cold medicine, just in case. It still did not fix the way I was feeling inside.

For the first time in my life, I felt as if nothing mattered. I had never known this kind of pain, nor had I the slightest idea of how to deal with it or turn how to it off.

My mother had taught Joni and me about love, respect, and a variety of other emotions. She had never taught us how to handle the pain of losing someone you loved or how to deal with the depression that followed. I guess that subject was too painful for her.

I had to force myself to enter my workplace. I did not want to pass the chattering do-rights that would also brand me with a big old red "A" if they knew my secret. I had fallen hard for someone else's husband.

Most of all, I dreaded running into Ronald or Marty first thing in the morning. After I've had about two cups of coffee, I could tolerate whatever they threw at me. But shit happens—there they were waiting as I opened my office door.

Ronald was seated behind my desk, and Marty was sitting on top of my desk, leaning towards Ronald. They both looked up at me, and so it began...

"Where you been this weekend, Ms. Vogue?" asked Marty, looking me up and down. Tracing me from head to toe with one finger.

"Not now, Marty. It is not a good time to poke mama bear." I pleaded.

"That's all right. We know where you were and who you were with," said Ronald.

"And how would you know that?"

"Marcus asked us where you would go if you wanted to get away for the weekend, and we told him you loved Biloxi. He also asked us what your favorite flower was. Plus, ya glowing. There's only one thing that can make a woman glow like that," said Ronald.

"Move! I yelled, pushing Ronald out of my chair. What do you two want?"

"Nothing. Marty bet me twenty bucks that if we asked you if you were with Marcus this weekend, you would lie and say no," stated Ronald.

"And she did," said Marty, snapping his finger, parading that, I- told-you-so, look on his face and doing that circular thing with his head that he does.

"First of all, you did not ask me if I were with Marcus. So, I did not lie. I didn't want to tell you either/or. And I still don't."

"Honey, that's called a discreet lie," said Ronald.

"That's not a lie of any sort. It is my way of keeping you two messy heifers out of my personal business."

"We are your business," whispered Marty.

"Is there anything else?" I asked.

Ronald took my hand and said, "Be careful. There is something not right about all this. I got a bad feeling."

"He got a bad feeling," said Marty snapping his fingers.

"What do you mean?" I asked.

"He means, watch your back. We heard that wife of his is a new age bitch," said Marty.

"Honey, pay attention to what is going on around you. I don't want to see you get hurt," Ronald said, practically pleading.

"*Too late*, I thought. It doesn't matter. I decided to end it between Marcus and me. So you don't have to worry about his wife."

"Good, cause I thought I was going to have to beat that bitch like she stole something if she came at you wrong," said Marty.

Marcus walked in, hearing 'stole something' and asked, "Who stole what?"

"Nobody stole anything. You two out!" I nearly shouted, pointing them in the direction of the door. They exited, giving Marcus that 'try-something' look, stare, and walk.

"Why are those two always so tetchy?"

"They are just being Ronald and Marty. You need something?"

"*Seulement toi*," Marcus said, closing the door behind him. Looking at him walk slowly toward me, with that sexy black man's walk, and licking his lips, took my mind off, Ronald and Marty.

He slid his hand down the side of my face. He rubbed my face gently with his thumb. Then he leaned in to kiss me. The other hand was pulling my blouse out of my skirt.

I was panting like a tigress in heat. I lay back on my desk, closed my eyes, and let my mind drift with thoughts of only Marcus and me, once again.

He fondled my breasts with both hands. His touch sent me into a daze. Lust was rushing to my head. Sweat was pouring out of my skin, and desire locked onto every orifice.

The knock on the door had us both rushing to fix ourselves, like two teenagers almost getting busted by one of their parents. He was wiping my lipstick off his lips and trying to conceal his hardness. I was rushing to put my clothes back together again.

Thank God, it was Monique, my intern, and not one of my permanents. Monique had this *thing* about herself that I noticed the first day she started at my company.

I had just made a pot of fresh coffee. After pouring himself a cup, Marty was about to take a sip when Monique seemed to sense that something was about to happen.

She held up her hand as though she was about to warn Marty but decided to put her hand down. I watched her as she seemed to regret, not speaking up.

As Marty put the cup to his mouth, he realized how hot it was. When he jerked the cup from his mouth, he spilled it on Avery, my printer, giving him a first-degree burn on the side of his face.

Monique put her head down as though she was sorry she did not say anything. I think I was the only one that noticed.

Since then, Monique would say or do truly mysterious things. That day, she looked at both of us with that witchy thing she does and instinctively knew something was going on.

She asked, "Would you like me to come back later?"

"Yes, in two hours," Marcus said.

I gave him a nudge and asked her if she needed anything. She had brought the poster designs for a new product we were working on. After she handed them to me, she walked out of my office with her head down, smiling.

I turned to Marcus and gave him that motherly stare, like when a child has done something wrong. "Don't say things like that. We cannot let those bleeding-hearts, do-gooders know about us," I scolded him.

"You think they don't know?" he said as he was walking out. Then he turned and asked if we were still on for Thursday night.

Thursday night was the night I planned to break off whatever it was Marcus and I had. He assumed it was another hot night of sex. It *was* going to be.

I was going to please him so well that he was never going to forget me. Afterward, I would free my conscience. I had to be with him one more time. Do-not-judge-me!

CHAPTER 30

Charlotte had called to invite me to lunch at her mini castle. I assumed that she wanted to tell me to back the hell off her husband.

I could have kicked myself for accepting her invitation. For all I knew, she was planning to make me disappear.

However, I needed to know what was on her mind. If I did not go to the pending tête-à-tête, curiosity would only eat at me, and I might regret it.

I could not help but feel a little jealous when the butler opened the door. In the foyer, I could see paintings by Armand Vartanian.

The price she paid for one of those paintings could have bought me two more condominiums. She had good taste - I had to give her that.

As I followed the butler into the living room, I saw a large family portrait of Marcus, Charlotte, and their two girls hanging over a huge fireplace. Why in

154

the hell did anyone need a walk-in fireplace?

That fireplace was the size of my bathroom or bigger. On the other side of her very large living room were expensive little Greek porcelain statues.

The center of the living room showcased a white Lavelle Melange double-sized sofa and white Lavelle Melange loveseat. In front of the sofa was a Trivellato antique coffee table.

To the side of the sofa was a white Brompton leather square cocktail ottoman, and hanging at her windows were white Neiman Marcus Lili Alessandra Mozart curtains. What she paid for those curtains would have kept me in shoes for a year.

The butler beckoned me to follow him. He escorted me to a screened-in patio and asked if he could get me anything to drink while I waited. Winch! Her butler waited on her hand and foot.

I started to say no, but knowing Charlotte, it could be a wait. She was about to confront the mistress, so she had to make herself look as good as possible. I asked the butler for a cup of hot tea. Maybe I should have asked for a double shot of brandy.

A few minutes later, the butler emerged, pushing a silver beverage stand. On the stand was a silver teapot and silver cups, on silver saucers, all on a silver platter. He set the platter on the table and left. Was I supposed to serve myself?

When Charlotte finally made her debut, I could not help but see why Marcus was so attracted to me. She had let herself go. It's a good thing the girl's got money.

She was nothing like the Charlotte I knew in high school and college. She had gained quite a bit of weight. Age had developed dark circles under her eyes, and time had replaced beauty with maturity.

I got the feeling she truly loved Marcus. When love is not shared, it can be painful. And, some women choose food for comfort. She looked as if she had been crying. I asked her what was wrong.

"I think you know what's wrong. Are you fucking my husband?" Charlotte asked.

That question did not surprise me, but I had thought we would chat a little, leading up to that question. But not Charlotte; she had to jump in head-first.

Well, I did not lie. "Yes, I am," I answered.

Then she got up and poured me a cup of tea. I noticed that silly smirk on her face and wondered if she had her butler to spike the tea in the teapot with succinylcholine.

You know, that shit that paralyzes you, but you are still conscious. Charlotte could do anything to me, and I would be awake to feel and see it all, but I would not be able to defend myself.

She noticed me looking in my cup and said, "There's nothing in it." I giggled a little at the thought of her seeming to read my mind.

"How long have you suspected something was going on with us?"

"Since we ran into you at Houston's'."

"I'd hoped as much. Did you ask Marcus if he was sleeping with me?"

"Yes, I did." And he denied it all."

"He did, huh?"

"Leave my husband alone."

"And miss the opportunity to hurt you, like you have hurt me in the past!"

"Go play with someone else's husband."

"But I like playing with your husband."

"Don't test me, Vikki!"

"Why, Charlotte, you can dish it, but you can't take it?"

"Dish what, Vikki?"

"Clyde Theard–Anthony Johnson ringing any bells?"

"That was college, Vikki."

Now, I could have let the situation defuse itself and walk away because it *was* college. We were both younger then but, revenge being like an oxymoron (bitter-sweet) and me being me, I had to add a touch of 'my kind of' sweetness to Charlotte's bitter ass attitude.

"You didn't even want them. You stole them to spite me. And, after you stole them from me, you dumped them."

"We were kids."

"Yeah, well, we're all grown up now, and I am stealing your man. And I am very much in love with him."

"But he's not yours to love, Vikki."

"You think a little piece of paper is going to stop me?"

Then she stood and gave me the evilest stare. I mean diabolical even for Charlotte.

"Go away, Lil side piece or your body parts will never be found."

"Is that a threat?"

"Of course, it is. One I intend on carrying out."

Okay, that threw me when she said *body parts*. She did not just say *body*. She said *body parts*. I wanted to tell her that I had already decided to leave her husband alone, but…since she had threatened me, well…

Then I stood, met her stare, and said, "When I'm done with him, I'll send him home." Then I purposely knocked over my cup of tea, spilling it on her Neiman Marcus Joy tablecloth.

If looks could kill, I would not have gotten that last roll in the hay with Marcus. Joni and my mother would have been planning my funeral.

What else could I do except wreak havoc in the world of Charlotte a little bit longer? After all, she had threatened me.

Then Charlotte had one last thing to say to me. "Go away, little girl, or I'll make you go away. You don't know what you are getting yourself into."

"Charlotte do not call me, little girl; you are one second older than me. And...Marcus likes *'little' girls,"* I said in an insolent tone as I walked away.

I know that *'little girl'* remark pissed her off—considering her size. I could feel her staring at me as I walked away. It made the hairs on the back of my neck stand. That bitch actually said *body parts*.

CHAPTER 31

I often thought about the threat Charlotte had made over the next few days and how disturbing it had sounded. Even that did not stop me from keeping my date with Marcus for one last sexcapade.

I needed to rush home to freshen up before his visit, but something was telling me to take my time. I should have listened.

When I walked into my apartment, I could sense something was off. I looked around, but everything seemed normal until I noticed my Lalique dolphin sitting on the countertop.

I just assumed I had put it there because, from time-to-time, I would take it out to admire it. As I was putting it back in the curio cabinet, I also noticed a book (Slaves With Benefits) that I thought I had left on my nightstand on the sofa.

Still, I thought, I did have three glasses of wine last night. I could have moved the book to the sofa. But when I went into my bedroom and saw my bra and panties that I had worn the day before on my body mirror, instead of in the clothes hamper, I started to become a little concerned about my frame of mind.

I had never put my undies on the mirror before. I placed my purse on the dresser and was walking toward the mirror to take them down when I felt a sharp pain in the back of my head.

***I was dreaming. Marcus and I were standing on the beaches of Biloxi, Mississippi, arguing. I had called him a 'ho,' and he had replied, "Maybe I was a 'ho' because I was searching for you." He always knew how to bring me down from one of my anger highs. ***

The constant ringing of my doorbell, the knocking, and my name called interrupted my sleep. At first, I was angry about someone waking me up and disturbing my dream of Marcus until I realized I was on the floor. My head was aching. What the hell had happened? Had I fallen and hit my head?

The room was so distorted that I staggered to the door. Thank God, it was Marcus. I had not expected him for another hour.

"You're early," I said, squinching my eyes in pain.

"No, I am not. I am right on time."

"What time is it?"

"It's nearly seven, miel."

"Seven? My head is throbbing."

"That old, I-have-a-headache cliché, huh?" asked Marcus

"Very funny!" I responded.

As I turned to walk away, Marcus noticed the blood on the back of my blouse and asked me what had happened. I felt the back of my head, looked at my hand, and nearly fainted when I saw my blood.

Marcus had to grab me to keep me from falling. He helped me on my sofa. I sat on the arm of my sofa, staring at the blood on my hand.

I told him I must have fallen and hit my head, holding the back of my head again. He moved my hand out of the way to look at the bruise.

"That's a *plaie méchant* babe," he said.

"Okay, during sex, I love it when you talk French. Right now, I need you to use your English vocabulary."

"Nasty wound."

"Okay."

Then he asked me to show him where I fell. I took him into the bedroom and showed him where I woke up on the floor.

"Mon amour, there is nothing here that would make that kind of *plaie."*

"Well it must be something because I have the *"plaie méchant"* to prove it," I said. Marcus seated me back on the sofa and went into the bathroom to get some peroxide and bandages to clean and cover my wound.

As Marcus went to open the medicine cabinet, he saw in through mirror the words *"la mort à putes,"* written in red.

The tone in his voice, when he called my name, was alarming. I walked to my bedroom door and noticed he was pointing. It was on the wall in my bedroom—over my bed.

"What does that mean?"

"Death to whores," Marcus said.

I cringed when he said it and nearly fell again. Marcus dialed 911. I grabbed my Glock.

CHAPTER 32

Before the police arrived, I told Marcus about the dolphin, the book, and my underwear. He was a little upset with me for not having told him that earlier.

I told him I hadn't said anything because I thought I had done those things and had just forgotten. As usual, I had wine.

Within the hour, my condo was swarming with N.O.P.D. Officers, Levy Police, Crime Scene Investigators, and Emergency Medical Technicians.

A nice-looking young detective questioned Marcus and me. A few police officers went door-to-door, asking my neighbors whether they had heard or seen anything suspicious.

The EMT that patched up my wound strongly suggested I go to the hospital and have my head examined. I was somewhat happy Marty was not around to hear that.

Marcus agreed with the EMT. "No, thank you, *Hospital* and *Vikki* don't even go in the same sentence," I said.

I looked over Marcus's shoulder and saw the CSI person laying out his equipment. He put swabs, tweezers, and tiny Ziploc bags on my kitchen counter. He also had a trajectory thingy to check for blood splatter in my bedroom.

Another CSI person was taking pictures of my bedroom wall with a digital camera, and another was dusting my dolphin, book, and body mirror for fingerprints.

"There was no forced entry, and the lock was not tampered with, sir," a Rookie Officer said to the detective.

My apartment was on the fourth floor, so there was no way anyone could have gotten in through the window.

Then that very attractive NOPD detective, named Johann Conway Jr., asked if I knew of anyone who would have it in for me.

Charlotte was my first thought, but I could not tell him that without admitting I was sleeping with her husband. Marcus worked for me, so that was the reason he was at my apartment. I would have said if Detective Conway had asked.

And I did not want Marcus to know about the meeting between Charlotte and me or the threat. There was no one else that I can remember.

Ronald and Marty, who lived two floors down from me, heard of my dilemma and rushed to be at my side.

Seeing Marcus, there spiraled their anger. The little prancing queen, Marty, started to question the police officers. Ronald asked, "How did they get in?"

I did not need to call the police I had Inspectors Do Little and Do Even Less to protect me.

Marcus put his hand under my chin and rubbed my jaw with his thumb; He asked if I were feeling better. I nodded, yes. I was so in love with that man.

His compassion, at a time like that, meant the world to me. Still, there was a heart that was going to be broken, and it was mine.

After the CSI technicians, the EMT's, the NOPD officers, and Levy police had gone, Marcus, Ronald, and Marty stayed behind. Marcus told Ronald and Marty that they could leave—that he would stay with me.

"Like that's gone happen," Marty said, walking to the sofa sitting down and clicking on the television. He sat back, propped, and crossed his legs on my coffee table, looking at Marcus with a goofy look, with Ronald next to Marty silently co-signing.

"Nervy, are they? You would think I did all of this," Marcus said.

"They are just overly protective as usual," I answered.

That night, Marcus spent the whole night with me. I slept in his arms. Ronald and Marty slept on the sofa bed. I could not begin to imagine what Marcus would tell Charlotte. Maybe he will say he was at the office all night.

I wished I could have been there. I would love to have heard what lie Marcus would tell Charlotte. Or, if she would believe it. Would they argue? Would she kick him out of the house?

She would not kick him out of their home because she knew he would come straight to me. Not the Duchess of dumb. She wasn't that dumb.

CHAPTER 33

I woke the next morning to the smell of bacon, eggs, and coffee. The scent of the coffee made me a little nauseous. Still, I wanted some, but Ronald had always gotten on me about not eating breakfast.

For me, breakfast was a cigarette and a cup of coffee or two. Ronald called it my Mexican breakfast. He was pleased that I had turned down coffee that morning.

As I watched Marcus putting on his shirt, I craved to have those Mandingo arms around me again—to feel him inside me again.

I could not help but love the men in my life. Marcus was risking his marriage to nurture me. Ronald and Marty were canceling their plans for the concert, to stay and protect me.

Marty stepped out into the hall to get the morning paper. We heard him scream like a banshee. All of us ran to the door to see why he was screaming. Marty pointed at the hall floor.

There was a knife lodged into the carpet, standing upright. It fell out of the newspaper Marty was holding and nearly impaled Marty's foot. Marty began to fan himself hysterically with his hands.

Ronald ushered Marty to the sofa and put his arms around the panicked princess. You would have thought the knife was for Marty, the way he carried on.

Hearing the screams, two of my neighbors were curious and opened their doors to see what the screaming was all about.

Mrs. Dayton was the first to open her door. The Pearson's were next. "Who's doing this? I yelled. They watched as Marcus steered me back inside, with one hand on my waist and the other seizing the knife.

"Things like this just don't happen in this neighborhood," said Mrs. Dayton, agreed with by the Pearson's.

When the Pearson's moved next door to me, nearly a year ago, I would speak to them whenever I saw them. Being neighborly, both would return the salutations.

Not long after, when I spoke to them, only the husband would speak back. I did not know what her problem was and did not care enough to try and find out.

Marcus sat the knife on the counter. Written in red on the handle was the word *"mort."* meaning death. I was pacing. It was not knowing who was doing those things to me; that was terrifying.

I was not a fearful person. In fact, I had been known to be fearless. But, that situation had sent my fear-o-meter from brave blue to cowardly yellow. Was I going to die? Was this person going to end my existence?

My head was spinning. Thoughts of my funeral passed darkly though my mind. Joni, my precious Joni, would be devastated. And my mother—would she blame herself for not being there to protect me.

That person was going to take me from people that loved me. I had downloaded a will document years ago, but I had never filled it out.

It is funny how you think you are going to live forever or have plenty of time. It seemed like my time was running out. I had begun to plan my demise. I filled out the will.

Ronald and Marty would continue to run my company. My mother and Joni were my insurance beneficiaries. My mother would inherit my condominium. She loved it. Would she even want it after I was gone?

Joni would finally get my painting *Forever Sisters*, (the only one of its kind) by Vera somebody, that she adored so much. She said she did not know why, but that painting reminded her of us, but much older—still joined at the hip.

I saw Ronald on the phone, talking to someone. I heard him say, "Marcus, the magnificent touched it, but the rest of

us were smart enough not to," giving
Marcus that 'yeah, you don nit look.'
Then I saw that look, Marcus gave
Ronald in return, and it was not a pretty
one.

CHAPTER 34

It was the same detective as before. Detective Johann Conway Jr. He had no more to add to the possibility of catching the culprit than he'd had the day before.

Detective Conway spoke with Marcus and Marty. Ronald was in the bedroom with me, trying futilely to comfort me. He tried cheering me up with anecdotes of our past experiences.

He started with, "Remember that time we were at a night club, and a portly woman came in dressed like a hoochie mama? She wore a short, tight-fitting dress that displayed each of her rows.

"You made a remark, thinking you had whispered it to Marty and me. But, when you have had one too many martinis, nothing is a whisper.

"You said, You know, big women should not wear dresses like that; it only makes them look cheesy. She heard and told on us. She turned out to be the wife of the owner of the club, and we got kicked out.

"Or the time when we got drunk and went to that exclusive dress store on Canal Street that is known for following 'only' black folks around.

"The plan was for you to look suspicious so the associate would follow you while Marty and I swiped a few things. I think we called that black man's justice.

"Or the time we were bike riding in City Park. There was a man that had parked his car and left his trunk open. Marty had released his hands from his bike handle-threw his hands in the air, and said, look y'all no hands," and he went flying into that man's trunk.

Nothing we reminisced about eased the distress that was weighing heavily on my mind. I had a bullseye on my chest and had no idea who was making me a target.

Marcus suggested he stay over another night. As much as I would have loved that, and knowing how much it would hurt Charlotte, I thought about his little girls and how much they must miss their father and sent him home.

That night, Ronald, Marty, and I sat in silence as we finished four bottles of Merlot. We all fell asleep in the living room.

Something woke me in the middle of the night. Ronald and Marty were both still asleep, snoring like roaring trains. Marty had one hand over Ronald's face, and Ronald was still holding a half-filled glass of wine.

I had gotten up to get a glass of water when I heard a noise coming from my bedroom. I tried waking Ronald and Marty, but they were too far gone. I walked slowly to my bedroom to investigate.

Even though my windows were closed, my white gown and hair were blowing. When did I change into my white gown? I could hear trees rustling with the wind, and those once mesmerizing drums that were so seductive when Marcus and I made love had begun to sound like funeral march drums.

Everything seemed so strange. My bedroom was glossy, and some of the content in my bedroom did not belong there.

It was as if I were somewhere else but at home. I could feel a presence in the room. I looked around and saw no one.

I noticed that I had left my Glock on my nightstand and rushed to get it. Before I could reach it, something penetrated my back four times.

I began to get weak as I staggered toward my nightstand. The room was getting dark. I could feel immense pain and something warm oozing down my back.

I marshaled the strength to turn and saw a figure holding something shiny. The last thing I remembered was that the figure wore a smile. Then darkness surrounded me.

I woke up drenched with sweat, checking myself for blood and wounds. I found it difficult to breathe. After a few seconds, my breathing regulated. My heart was still beating so fast I thought it was going to pop out of my chest.

My mind was racing with thoughts of my dream. Who was that person? What could I have possibly done for that person to want me dead?

Fear took a stance that would not bend, even after I realized it was just a dream—or was it an omen?

CHAPTER 35

Ronald and Marty both suggested we take the day off and go shopping. Shopping was second to alcohol when it came to relieving stress for us.

Oakwood Mall was packed with shoppers searching for Halloween costumes. Marconi's (our favorite stress relief store) had a sign indicating shoppers could buy one and get another of equal value for .50 percent% off.

One of the posters had a couple of black teenage girls skating. The store had dressed them in sports gear. That one was supposed to sway you toward the sports floor. It reminded me of the times Joni, I, and our friends would meet up at the skating rink.

I had not told Joni or my mother of my current situation. Joni would worry herself to death. My mother would want to move in to protect me, that I did not want. My mentally strenuous, over shielding, and overbearing mother would drive me insane. She would quote the bible to everyone that came to my door.

Then I thought if something did happen to me, would they be angry at me for not telling them. Would my mom and Joni ever forgive me? Catch 22.

I heard Marty scream. My knees got so weak I could barely stand. I began to tremble with fear. I ran to his aid, only to learn he had finally found a pair of genuine white leather pants that he could afford.

I was happy that he had found the pants and was not screaming about being attacked. I was angry at him for scaring the shit out of me. So, I gave him a pop on his arm that should have left a nasty *plaie.*

"Ouch! Bitch," Marty said.

"Serves you right, for screaming like that. You know Vikki *scarred,*" smirked Ronald. Ronald almost got the second pop.

After we had exhausted ourselves with shopping, we headed for the food court. I cannot explain why, but after we were seated, I got that eerie feeling again that someone was watching us.

Was this what I had become? A petrified damsel-in-distress with paranoia as a chaser? Would I ever be able to stay in my apartment alone again?

Ronald and Marty could not babysit me forever. And I couldn't expect Marcus to abandon his little girls whenever I needed him.

CHAPTER 36

A month had passed with no more incidents of terror. I figured whoever had been stalking me had moved on, gone to jail, died, or found someone else to frighten.

Marcus had called and said he would swing by at seven. It was nearly seven when I took a shower, brushed my teeth, put on something sexy, and sprayed myself with my "Happy" cologne, his favorite.

That day was going to be the last time Marcus would polish my bed with his essence. I was giving up the love of my life. It was the hardest thing I had ever done, and probably the hardest thing I will ever do.

His contract would be up soon, and I had decided it was best not to hire him permanently. It was a decision I had made not so lightly.

I greeted him at the door, wearing my red fishnet onesie that revealed everything I had to offer. I wore my red stiletto heels and my hair down.

"Wow!" he said.

Pleased at his 'wow,' I took his hand and led him into the living room. I helped him peel off his shirt, button by impressive button. While kissing him erotically, I sat him down on the sofa and got on my knees.

Dear God, please be merciful and send me another Marcus, only single. I licked my lips as I looked at his firm male organ. Not too big and, mercy not small. A perfect fit. I ran my hands down his chest in anticipation. Just the thought of doing him was getting me wet.

I could not help but wonder if Charlotte realized the value of her husband. Did she neglect him—ignore his needs, make him feel like a commodity instead of her better half?

Knowing what we were about to do and that it could never happen again, I had to make this last time count. I needed him always to remember me.

I traced his chest with one hand, and the other slid up and down his arm. 'How can I muster the strength to walk away from this spectacular specimen?' I thought.

I put both hands around his neck and began to kiss him eagerly. My tongue fondled his neck to his chest, teasing his chest hairs, moving slowly down his stomach to his groin. He closed his eyes, quivered, and moaned in delight.

I removed his pants and jockey shorts and held his male hardness in my hand. His face gleamed of ecstasy. As I seduced his erection with my tongue, I could feel him getting harder in my hand.

He grabbed my hair to guide my way and encouraged my head to meet his gestures. His breathing became erratic. His grip on my hair was tightening.

He was panting like a lion in heat and welcomed the attention in that area. His stride was in rhythm with my mouth as I ventured up and down on his male erectness.

My tongue spun slowly around the head of his stiffness, giving him added and vast satisfaction, followed by several strokes coaxed by my lips. I pulled out so my tongue could slowly trace his outline.

My lips lapped around his penis, slurping in and out, up and down, causing his brain to malfunction with pleasure until he could not hold back his release. He wanted that release inside me.

He began to tremor as he pulled me up to him. He lifted me in his arms, and I wrapped my legs around his waist as he carried me to the bed. He unzipped my onesie and stood in awe of all that I was giving him.

He lay on top of me and slid his penis inside me. My body wanted all of him. As he thrust himself inside slowly, tenderly, lovingly, I felt a wonderful explosion in me.

His lips kissed their way to my neck, while his hand caressed my breast as we moved to each other's pace.

I lifted my hips higher for him to be able to penetrate as deep as my body would allow. I squirmed slowly under him. He grabbed one of my legs to lift it even higher so I could feel all of him. He probed deeper and deeper inside me with every thrust.

I flipped him over and climbed on top. Pleased with my dominance, he grew even harder. I rode him with confidence. He cuddled my breast while sliding one finger in my mouth. strode

I closed my lips around his finger, allowing my tongue to twirl around it. Our strides became rapid. Our breathing was intense. Our bodies drenched each other with sweat.

The room began to spin wildly. I could hear the music of those distant erotic drums again. They were beating slowly and more sensually.

It began to rain. Lightning lit up my bedroom like New Year's Eve, and when the thunder cried out, so did we. We reached our climaxes in unity.

I looked down at him and began to cry at the thought of never feeling this way again. He wiped away my tears with his thumbs. The way he looked at me, he knew this would also be his last.

We lay in bed, holding each other for what seemed like an eternity. Neither of us said a word.

He could feel the warmth of my tears as they rolled off my face and onto his chest, and he said," "It's okay, *mon amour,* I understand. I can't expect you to put your life on hold waiting for me.

After Marcus had left, I crawled back onto my bed, tear-staining my pillows for the remainder of the night. My heart started to feel like it had no viable purpose to serve.

As I walk the shores of yesteryear, remembering what once was, I feel your presence on every grain, of sand that tasted our love.

You planned on a love that's short but sweet, yet not with infinite time, nor did you plan our souls to meet, or on love so sweet and kind.

The shore so cold and lonely still, with its misty morning dew, I wonder if you're missing me, for I am so missing you.

CHAPTER 37

The next day, I called Joni and told her it was over between Marcus and me. Joni was glad to hear it, but I still could not stop the tears from falling. Hearing my cries, she said she was on her way.

It is almost like Ronald and Marty can sense when I am in pain. Ronald had called to see if I wanted some company. Before I could say anything, my cries said it all.

"We're only twenty minutes away, baby girl," said Ronald.

I was standing at the window watching the rainfall again, but the showers that fell outside did not compare to the waterworks inside my heart. I was in so much pain. I felt like a part of my soul had been taken from me.

If only Marcus had told me he was married before I had slept with him or had fallen in love with him, I would not be standing here feeling like tomorrow was just a waste of space.

I knew to end the relationship was the right thing to do. But I would never forget what we had. I wondered if I would ever connect with another man as I had with Marcus. That kind of love only comes once in a lifetime. Damn my mother for raising me with Christian principles!

I began to wonder if Marcus felt the same about me, as I did him. I remembered my mother saying once that when cupid shoots his arrows, sometimes it does not hit both people.

That leaves one person in love, and the other is not. I wondered if cupid's arrow had hit me and missed Marcus, leaving me in love all by myself.

Joni arrived at the same time as Ronald and Marty. I could hear the commotion in the hall just outside my door. I opened it to see Joni and Marty about to rip each other a new one. When Ronald saw me, he shushed them both.

They all came toward me, smiling as though the argument in the hall had never taken place or that I did not see it.

Joni and Marty were shoving each other to enter first. I guessed the first one to enter was the better one.

Marty poured Ronald, himself, and me a glasses of wine. When Joni asked where her glass was, Marty said, "Today is not Communion."

Even though Joni found no humor in what Marty had said, Ronald and I laughed amused. I needed that laugh. A minute ago, I had thought I would never laugh again.

Joni got up to pour herself a glass of wine, but not before popping Marty upside his head. "Watch it now; I will smack the hell out of a Christian too!" Marty said.

"This is too much for anyone to have to deal with," I said, with the tears falling like Niagra Falls.

An unexpected reply came from Marty. He said, "sometimes God gives us more than we can handle to test our strength. You take it day-by-day. Each day it will become easier to handle than the last day. We'll be here for you. We ain't going nowhere."

We picked up our glasses and headed for the patio. I was horrified to see someone had broken all my potted plants and scattered them all over the place.

Someone had cut up my patio furniture and written "adulterous bitch" in red paint on my imitation grass.

Joni wanted me to call the police, but I told her there was little to nothing they could do at this point. Whoever it was doing those things was meticulous. He or she never left fibers, fingerprints, or anything that could lead the police to identify him or her.

Joni gave me that, hold up—wait a minute—what-the-hell look and asked, "How long has this been going on?"

"A few months!"

"A FEW MONTHS AND YOU DID NOT TELL MOM OR ME! Mom is going to be so pissed at you, Joni said while picking up her cell phone. She said, "I'm telling!," as she began to dial our mother's phone number.

I grabbed Joni's hand and pleaded with her not to tell our mother. "Please don't tell her. I did not want to worry you two."

"This is not something you keep from people who love you, Vikki."

Marty walked over and whispered in Joni's ear: "*I knew.*" Then he walked away, feeling superior.

"This is not the time, tinker bell," said Joni.

Joni wanted me to call the police, but I told her that it would not do any good—they had nothing. Then she said, "The more calls you make to them, the stronger your case will be if you have to kill the bastard."

I had to take a step back because this is my little Christian sister giving me advice on subjects she should not be familiar with.

It truly made sense, but I did not want to seem like a helpless female who was afraid of her own shadow, calling the police every time I heard a pin drop. Besides, I had my good friend Glock to protect me, if I could get to it, I thought, remembering my dream.

After nearly an hour of cleaning and talking, I made everyone go home. They were worried about leaving me alone. I was afraid to be alone, but I forced myself to man-up or woman-up.

CHAPTER 38

I decided to take a little time off to get my head together and to try to figure out who was behind all of this.

Charlotte was the first to come to mind again. She had the grade "A" motive. I had slept with and fallen in love with her husband.

But how had she gotten into my apartment? How had her big-ass gotten passed, Jason? I honestly could not bring myself to believe it was Charlotte. She would not risk going to jail and leaving those little girls behind.

When I was over at their mansion, one of the little girls had fallen and scraped her knee. I noticed how attentive Charlotte was to her daughter.

Anyone with that kind of passion would not have done something like that to me or any other woman. Maybe she knew Marcus didn't love her. A woman's hurt or her jealousy is a very powerful emotion that frequently leads to an uncontrollable rage.

Most times, the combination of the two overrules her better judgment. That can be very dangerous for whoever is on the receiving end of that rage.

Or, it could have been one of my old boyfriends. They also had motives. I was the dumper, not the dumped. Maybe one of my exes decided to get a little revenge for me breaking his heart.

They each had something missing, something I needed. Marcus was the only man that had ever filled that something, and he had to be a married man, someone I couldn't have. Married to a bitch, I could not stand.

Whoever it was, he or she was good—really good. That person, not only, got pass the doorman, but got into my apartment, and never left a clue. I thought about hiring a private detective or a bodyguard to stand outside my door.

But then I thought if my harasser saw a bodyguard or got wind of a PI sniffing around, he might move on, and some other poor woman would have to endure that madness.

I wanted that bastard caught even if I had to put myself in harm's way. That feeling of being the lamb tied to the stake came to mind.

I did not like the helpless way I was feeling. I was not eating or sleeping, getting constant headaches, and I was having nightmares. I felt depressed all the time and rarely left my apartment. Losing Marcus added to my state of being.

The only good thing that came out of that was that I had lost a few pounds. I could finally fit into that black mini skirt that I'd had hanging in my closet for motivation.

My world was crumbling in front of me. Was this my penance for sleeping with a married man and loving it? If it was, I humbly begged God to forgive me.

I explained to God that I had not asked for forgiveness before because I knew I was going to do it again, and again, and again.

My mother used to say that God forgives us for our past sins but sin no more. And…since I knew I was going to keep on doing it, I didn't ask for forgiveness.

One must think of God's powers or commandments as being inconsequential to ask him for forgiveness for the same sin over and over again.

CHAPTER 39

After a few weeks of retreating and no more incidents, I decided to go back to work. All of my staff had heard what had happened (thanks to Marty) and were very sympathetic.

My employees offered a wide range of comfort, from a place to stay so I would not be alone—to getting one of their relatives that dabbled in voodoo to put a curse on the unsub—one offered a friend that could make my stalker disappear without a trace.

All of the offers were sweet, but I had to decline them all. I thanked everyone, and we returned to work as usual.

Avery came to me and offered a special condolence. He told me he had a cousin that went through the same thing; only she was killed. That was something my ears were begging to hear.

Then I saw Marcus. He was standing there with so much empathy in his eyes that I wanted to run to him. I did not, so stop judging!

Then we gave each other that pitiful look, put our heads down, and walked away. It was as though we were both ashamed of what we had done. Or we were both sorry it had to end. My vote was on sorry.

When I unlocked my office door and walked in, there were a dozen long-stemmed black roses in the center of my desk. Someone had shoved everything else on the floor.

The portrait of my mother, Joni, and I was torn to shreds. The sofa that Marcus and I had made out on— lots of times—was cut in several spots. This mysterious person knew where I worked. That person can get to me anywhere.

I just stood there in disbelief. Marty saw me just standing there and came over.

"What the fuck happened in here?" Marty asked.

"Watch your language in the office, Marty," I demanded.

"My bad. What the fuck happened here?" Marty said again in a whisper.

"You dick!" I said, shoving him.

He said it loud enough, the first time that Marcus and several other employees had heard. Marcus ran towards me, shoving his way through the crowd. When he saw the mess in my office, he also stood in disbelief.

He ordered everyone to go back to work, and he closed my office door. He sat me in the conference room and called the police.

Then he came to me. Marcus said, "I know it's over, but I can't leave you at a time like this, even if it jeopardizes my marriage."

That is what I wanted to hear from him, but I could not allow him to put his marriage at risk for me any longer.

I also understood that if I spent any more time with Marcus, I would regret my decision to let him go. I would be stuck loving someone else's husband, decreasing my chances of getting a husband of my own.

I thanked him and told him the police were going to handle it. He said those memorable words to me again: "Okay, I'm here if you need me." Just knowing he was there for me, was enough.

CHAPTER 40

Marcus had made an executive decision and sent everyone home for the day before the police arrived, except Ronald and Marty. He could not have gotten rid of those two if he'd tried to bribe them to leave the building.

Just as at my apartment, my office swarmed with NOPD officers, Levy police, and CSI technicians. Only this time, EMT's were not necessary. I had officially become a stalked victim.

Detective Johann Conway Jr. brought with him his uncle and partner Detective Lavar Damian. Damian had just come back to work after taking an extended leave. Conway was the lead detective and had filled Damian in on my case.

Damian had worked several stalker cases before Conway had joined the force. He began by telling me why some women get stalked and what I could do to protect myself.

Detective Damian said, "Most stalkers are men, young to middle-aged. It could be an ex or someone that sees you every day and has developed a fixation for you. Every stalker has a personal M.O."

"What's an M.O.?" asked Ronald.

"M.O. means Modus Operandi," said Detective Conway.

"What's a modus operandi?" asked Marty.

"The way the perp does things."

"Well, speak English then. I swear it's like listening to Marcus. Can't understand a damn thing he says," said Marty.

After giving Marty an irritated grunt, Detective Conway added that each stalking case is different, making it hard to catch the perps. Hence, personal M. O. Unless the victim knows the stalker, the police do not usually catch him or her until it is too late.

"Too late for what?" asked Marty.

"Too late to help the victim."

"By too late, you mean he kills her?"

"Sometimes, yes, said Damian. He or she will try to intimidate or threaten the victim and when that fails, it almost always turns to violence."

"So, this is a no-win for me, right?" I asked.

"Not necessarily, said Detective Conway. I noticed you have a Glock on your nightstand. Always keep it with you. Get security cameras for your apartment.

"Make sure they are on, whether you are home or not. Get a dog if you like dogs. Tell your neighbors what is going on. Alert the doorman. And, most importantly, spend as little time alone as possible. He or she needs you to be alone."

Marty said, "That's it; we're moving in!"

"Bull shit! I will not live like a victim, and I won't be a prisoner in my own home, and I won't share my apartment with you two prissy bitches," I said firmly.

"That's the spirit, and don't be afraid to use that gun. As you have seen, stalkers are usually very clever and seldom leave any clues," Detective Conway said as he walked off.

I noticed Conway and Damian's physique as they left and thought if only I had met Damian before I fell for Marcus. If only I were ten years younger for Conway.

"Uhhhh, no, she didn't say she don't want us here," said Marty.

"I believe she did," Marcus whispered in Marty's ear. The look on Marty's face could have brought down an empire.

"Uhhhh, Mr. 'think you all that,' she said you can't stay here either," said Marty with that right-back-at-you attitude.

While those two were going at it, I remembered Joni telling me her husband had a friend that owned a video supply store. I called her and asked for the location. She said she would meet me there.

CHAPTER 41

The video shop was located in the center of Canal Street, which marked the heart of the bowl-shaped New Orleans.

I had not been shopping on Canal Street since before Katrina. I noticed a lot had changed as I drove down Canal Street, crossing Broad Street.

There was one thing that was still constant: shoppers. When I saw the number of shoppers, I could not believe the country was in a recession.

The sign outside the red brick building read: I Got My 👁 On You Electronics. Clever, I thought. The little bell ding-a-ling-ed to alert the owner that someone had entered his establishment.

From behind a partition emerged a beautiful man. I almost forgot why I came into the store. He was definitely a Marcus substitute. *Please let him be single.*

Joni walked in just as I was about to tell the owner what it was that I needed. I turned to greet her, hugging her.

"Hi, Mark," Joni said, hugging him. "This is my sister, Victoria; she is the one I told you about," Joni said- pointing at me.

I want a hug, too!

"Vikki," I said, holding my hand out. Had I imagined he had squeezed my hand a little? Was that a signal?

"Are you married, single, or gay?" I asked.

"Vikki! Joni protested giving me a shove.

"Single, not married, not gay," Mark answered with a smile on his face.

"Great! I replied. You won't know if you don't ask," I whispered to Joni.

After I told Mark what it was that I needed, he suggested three wireless cameras because of the rooms in my condominium.

He also suggested infrared sensors so the system would record even at night, in case my power accidentally or purposely went out.

Mark handed me a pamphlet with instructions on how to view my home from any computer, wherever I was.

He also showed me illustrations on how to hook up my new electronic bodyguards—since I had turned down his invitation to install them for me—and he advised me on the best places to put them.

Because I had two doors, the first camera would be pointed directly at the one in the living room, and that camera would cover the entire living room, dining area, patio door, and kitchen.

The second would be in my bedroom that covered my bedroom and bathroom.

The third would be in the hall outside my apartment covering my front door and the elevator.

I lived on the fourth floor, so I did not think anyone could get in through the patio doors. I seldom locked them, until now that is.

He gave me his card and said I could call him day or night. When all of this is over with, and I if am still alive, maybe I will give him a call. Had God opened a big-ass window for me?

Maybe God had forgiven me for my past sins with Marcus and sent me a duplicate Marcus.

When we left the store, I noticed a hooded person across the street with his or her back to us, seemingly looking in the shop window. Then it appeared to be texting.

That eerie feeling crept up on me again. Joni noticed me looking across the street and asked me what it was that I was looking at, and I turned to answer her. When I looked back across the street, the person was gone.

Had I imagined the hooded figure? With everything that was going on, it would be no wonder.

"You wanna grab some lunch?" asked Joni.

"Not now. I want to get home and install these cameras."

***

Loving a Married Man

The male unsub had sent the female unsub a video of Vikki entering a video store. "Does she think a few generic ass cameras are going to save her stupid ass?" the female unsub said, speaking to the male unsub.

The female unsub had been on the phone ordering supplies for her big day. Using her ex-husbands pass-code and license, she was able to log into pharmaceutical companies, with no questions asked.

She ordered four infusions of ketamine. One surgical scalpel. All-purpose tourniquets. Disposable gloves. Two bags of Baxter Viaflex Intravenous fluid. Four hundred milligrams of Modafinil, Fifty milligrams of Acepromazine and Two operating tables. Her next stop was the hardware store. She needed a box of heavy-duty garbage bags, rope, and ten-cylinder blocks.

***

CHAPTER 42

When Joni and I got back to my apartment, I got that feeling again. That feeling that I should run.

Joni looked around the room and noticed that someone had slashed the painting of *'Forever Sisters.* That was the only thing in my apartment that had been desecrated.

Joni said, "Okay, now I am pissed.

***One summer, Joni came to visit me at Stanford. I showed her off to all my classmates. Most of all, I showed her off to California. I took her to the Cantor Arts Museum in Silicon Valley.

Just outside the museum was a woman selling art she had painted herself. One was called "Forever Sisters." The painting was of two older women sitting together, and they were laughing. When Joni saw *'Forever Sisters,'* she said I should buy it, because that would be us when we got old-always together.***

The painting itself was not of any value, but its sentimental value was priceless. So, you can imagine her fury when she witnessed its destruction. I was shocked to hear her use such words.

"Should we call the police?" Joni asked.

"No, not this time. These cameras are all the police we need."

The computer was set up in my dining room. We set up the cameras and pointed one in the corner of my living room. We put the second one in my bedroom and the third out in the hall.

Then we loaded information into my computer. Voilà! There was my living room, my kitchen, my bedroom, and the hall. From the angle of the camera in my bedroom, we could see into my bathroom.

My system was also set up to alert me when someone entered my home–the speakers would start to beep. I asked Joni to walk into the living room to see if it worked.

As she entered the living room, my speakers started beeping. She walked into my bedroom, and I could see her clear as day.

All angles were covered. I even called Jason and asked him to change the locks on my door. I briefed him on what was going on. I also reached out to a few of my neighbors.

Then Joni went home, and I drove to my office to see if I could view my apartment room from there. It worked.

Now we play the waiting game.

CHAPTER 43

I was seated at my desk, looking out of the window, wondering why all of this was happening to me?

All things happen for a reason, Joni had said. What reason could there possibly be for this? Why is this part of God's immaculate plan?

I was not a bad person. I may have been a little warped around the edges, but who wasn't? Be honest. If you don't have a little crazy in you, something is seriously wrong.

I didn't think I deserved this. I knew sometimes God wanted to reach down from heaven and smack the hell out of me for my sins. But why this?

Joni used to make a joke about me when I would face Judgment Day. She said I would be standing at the pearly gate, waiting to go in, and God would say, "You can't come up here." God would call Satan and tell him that he was sending me down there, and Satan would tell God, "Oh, hell no! She can't come down here either!"

Marcus knocked on my office door lightly as I was deep in thought and smiling at what Joni had said. "Can I come in?" he said. I told him to come in, even though I still did not completely trust myself alone with him.

He had been working with Ronald and Marty on the new project, and I must say I was impressed.

There was a company that was being sued for selling faulty baby dolls. Our project was to focus on damage control.

It was up to my team and me to show the world that those baby dolls were no longer a threat. And the new materials Marcus showed me proved to do just that.

He also brought with him sectors on where and when we should promote the dolls the most. It was nearing Christmas, so time was crucial.

He moved closer to me, and my heart started to beat rapidly. Those little beads of lust oozed their way out of my pores again.

That feeling of sexual hunger came rushing into my head. I began to feel a faint coming on. I had to hurry to the bathroom and splash water on my face.

"You can't have him," I continually tried to convince myself.

When I returned to my office, he was leaning on my desk with his arms folded and legs crossed. Like the time when I followed him home, and he beat me back to my condominium.

I froze at how striking that man was. All the times we had made love were roaming through my mind at once. It was a kaleidoscope of pleasure. I wanted to do him right there, on my desk. Again, and again, and again.

After clearing my throat, I asked, was there anything else? He said, "No, ma'am, and walked away.

"Okay, then. I'll get back to you later."

He turned and gave me a seductive smile, accompanied by that hypnotizing stare thing that he does. That stare alone curled my toes.

I watched as he slowly walked away with that proud black man's walk. Those jeans were fitting him so well I wanted to grab a handful of his ass–*ets*.

I couldn't help but admire his strong brawny back and shoulders that I used to glide my hands up and down during sex, or just because I could.

I'd hoped Mark would be as good in bed as Marcus was—if I ever got to sleep with him before being murdered.

It would make giving up my black treasure tolerable. Then I would not need to think dreadful things about Marcus to get him out of my system.

You know what we do, ladies. We think of the way he walks and how it irritates us. The way he talks that causes us to tune him out. And, the way he chews his food, that makes us want to barf. It may all be superficial, but it helps.

You do whatever it takes to get a man out of your system. But there was nothing wrong with Marcus. He was damn near perfect.

CHAPTER 44

The parking lot where we parked our cars embraced the evening sun with a vengeance. So, I always parked my car toward the back under a huge magnolia tree.

I looked up at the sky and saw that the moon was playing peekaboo with the clouds. The weatherman had said a severe thunderstorm was headed our way. I rushed to my car. I was in a hurry to get home before the rain started.

It was dark on the path to where my car was parked. Most of the lights in the lot had blown out, and because of the wind blowing, the others were blinking, getting ready to blow out.

The lightning struck a power line, causing the remaining lights to make popping sounds and die one by one. I could hear the sounds and see the sparks light up the areas where sparks fell.

The last light remaining was right over my car. I thought, At least I'll be able to see the keyhole on my car. I'd wished I had one of those little flashlight key chains.

I had worked late that night, and so had Marcus. Marcus offered to walk me to my car. Foolish me, I turned him down. I was still trying to keep that distance.

I'm sure the walk to my car would have felt like he was walking me home from school. It would have been too romantic to ignore the gist.

Also, having Marcus walk me to my car would scare off my predator if he was out there. Even though I had good reason to be afraid, I would not allow myself to succumb to fear. I put on my big girl panties and walked briskly to my car.

Something was telling me to go back inside and ask Marcus to walk me no matter what I felt. You would have thought I would have learned to listen to that little voice in my head by now.

I got that feeling of being watched again. I looked around, but no one was there. Then I heard what sounded like a twig snapping.

That time, when I turned, there was that hooded figure. It looked like the same hooded figure that I saw on Canal Street, and it was standing near my car.

I froze with fear. The figure just stood there. It was taunting and frightening me. I could not move. It did not move. It was like a Mexican stand-off.

My heart was racing; sweat began to roll down my face and back. I tried to scream, but nothing came out.

Why didn't the person move toward me? Why was he or she just standing there? "My gun," I thought. I reached frantically inside my purse. I pulled it out and aimed my gun in his direction, but he was gone.

The wind began to change and blow with more force separating flowers, leaves, and branches from the Magnolia tree. Little speckles of rain began to fall, disfiguring my vision.

I was alone and vulnerable, in the dark, with the person that wanted me dead. I wiped my eyes, trying to stay focused. I spun around, desperately searching for him.

I heard a big bang like an explosion, and then all the lights on the street went out. It was pitch-black. The moon provided enough light for me to see the figure had retreated.

I was there, for God knows how long, pointing my gun in every angle of the parking lot — waiting for that person to reappear. The rain began to pour. I was getting soaked. All of a sudden, I could not move. ?

Then I felt hands on me. I began to scream uncontrollably. I started beating the hooded person with my gun. I fought with vigor and everything else I had in me. I was punching, scratching, and kicking. I was not going down without a fight.

"Calmez-toi, Cherie," Marcus said, trying to stop me from kicking his ass while pulling me closer to him. It was a good thing my gun was on safety. I shuddered to think about how I might have shot Marcus.

I was shaking with fear. I looked into Marcus' eyes and began to feel safe. I could feel his heart beating as I laid my head on his chest.

I needed his strong arms to embrace me and wash away my fears. I just wanted him to hold me forever. I knew it was over between us, but at that moment in time, he was all mine.

We walked back into the building. Marcus sat me down on the sofa in my office. I had forgotten to thank him for taking charge and ordering new furniture for my office. Especially a big enough sofa that we could pound on all day.

He wrapped a towel around me and made me a cup of tea. I was still shaking and totally freaked out. That was too close for comfort.

"What happened?" Marcus asked, sitting next to me.

"I was walking to my car when I looked up and noticed the lights started going out one-by-one like that movie, "House On Haunted Hill. When Vincent Price was in the cellar, and the lights went out one-by-one."

I don't know what made me think of that movie, but those lights going out like that movie scared the bejesus out of me.

Then, I told him about the hooded phantom on Canal Street how the hooded stranger was there one minute and gone the next. When I looked down, from the lights, I thought the same figure was in the parking lot.

"I did not see anyone," he said.

"I did not imagine it, Marcus, he was there," I said in a slightly elevated tone.

"Calmez-toi, I'm here for you now," he said, pulling me closer to him-rubbing my arm. My heart did not want to release that Maverick of a man. "True love never dies; it lies dormant," came to mind.

I was still loving him. But my mind had to remind my heart that he was still married and not mine to love.

CHAPTER 45

Later that night, I dreamed of my grandmother. I was standing in the midst of an deserted building. I had never been in or seen this building before. The surroundings were not familiar to me at all.

Clusters of debris covered most of the floor. The was an elevator and signs that read stairs. It was so quiet I could hear my heartbeat as I walked slowly down one side of the building. Even the rats that were moving about, didn't make a sound.

The mist inside the building was so thick I could barely see. At the end of that hall, my grandmother, who had been dead for almost eleven years, was standing there. I wanted to run to her, but I could not move. Then she spoke to me.

"Remember the argument, child," she said.

"What argument?" I asked.

"Remember the woman."

"For God sake's gram, just tell me, what argument, what woman?"

"Don't trust him."

"Don't trust whom?"

"You need to wake up now, love. Remember," my grandmother said as she backed into the mist.

"Jesus Gram. What argument? What woman? Do not trust whom? Remember what? WHAT ARE YOU TRYING TO TELL ME! WHY IS IT THAT DEAD PEOPLE ALWAYS COMMUNICATE IN RIDDLES?! I yelled, but she was gone.

I woke up, saturated in sweat, frantically looking around my bedroom. I looked as if I had just stepped out of the shower wearing my nightgown. I had to get up and change my clothes and my sheets.

Was the woman she warned me about, Charlotte? Charlotte and I had a discussion. It was not an argument. However, she did threaten to cut me into pieces.

Loving a Married Man

Could the man be Marcus that I should not trust? But why would Marcus want to harm me? I can't think of anyone else. Maybe it was Charlotte because I was screwing her husband? Maybe it was Marcus because I ended our affair?

That dream had given me another Goddamn headache, so I went to the bathroom to get some aspirins. I had not realized I had left my bathroom light on.

I looked at myself in the bathroom mirror. I was as pale as a ghost. And that's saying something for a sista. I looked ten years older than I was.

This fear has got to stop. *It* will be the death of me. For days, I had been checking my computer to see if anyone had been in my home. No one. Nothing.

Just out of curiosity, I went to my computer to do my usual check, thinking it would be nothing, again. There it was. *"Flagrante delicto!"* Finally, I would see who was stalking me.

As I watched the video, I nearly fell out of my seat. That person walked across my living room. Where did the hooded person come from? Why didn't the cameras catch him walking through the door?

I quickly turned to make sure the person was on the computer and not in my living room behind me.

I watched in horror as that hooded person seemed to be the same one on Canal Street and in the parking lot. Then he or she walked toward my bedroom. It stood at my bedroom door for the longest time, watching me sleep.

Why hadn't the sensors beeped to let me know someone was in my home? You just lost ten brownie points, Mark. Why was it just standing there watching me sleep?

The figure walked around to the side of my bed and tilted its head to one side. If that person wanted me dead, that would have been the time to do it.

The figure went into my bathroom and turned on the light. First, the figure slapped my shower curtain for no apparent reason. Then figure opened my medicine cabinet and looked at my vitamin bottles.

Then it went into my kitchen, opened the refrigerator, bending slightly, as if trying to decide what to cook for dinner. Then the person grabbed a bottle of orange juice, then disappeared in the living room as suddenly as it had appeared.

Where did the figure go? Is he or she still in my home? I did a quick sweep of my bedroom, and no one was there. Then I practically ran to my nightstand to grab my Glock.

CHAPTER 46

It was obvious the figure did not want me dead at that moment. It had ample time to kill me. What was it waiting for? Where did it go?

I called Ronald and Marty. I wanted so badly to call Marcus, but he had risked enough helping me.

Within minutes, Ronald and Marty arrived. Marty burst through the door with a baseball bat in his hand, dressed in a Santa-Claus-printed onesie, yelling, "Where that mother-fucker at?"

"Oh, Lord, how ya doing, girl?" Ronald asked as he pranced in behind Marty, giving me a reassuring hug.

"He's gone," I said.

"He better be. You know I got you, girl," said Marty, still looking around the room.

"What are you wearing?" I asked Marty.

"You like this?" Marty asked, bending over and putting his index finger on his lips, attempting to be sexy.

"Yes, I do; I do."

"Tell us what happened, please, before Marty starts modeling for you."

"He was here in my apartment watching me sleep," I began. I told them I'd had a bad dream and when I woke up, I went to the computer and there he was.

"Girl, you do a lot of dreaming. And it is always bad dreams. Do you ever have good dreams?" asked Marty.

"Shut up," I said timidly to Marty.

"Hold up! He saw you sleeping, and he didn't run out of your apartment?" said Marty.

I looked at Marty and gave him an I-could-fuck-you-up-right-now look, but despite his antics, Marty had my back more than anyone else.

"I turned on the computer to finally see who it was, but he was hooded, and I did not recognize that person at all. I couldn't tell you if it was a man or a woman."

"Why would you turn on the computer?" Marty asked.

"I have a camera system now, and it's connected to the computer."

"Oh, shit, I'm on CCTV," Marty said.

"Shut up, Marty," Ronald nearly shouted.

"Tell me to shut up again, and I'm gone tell her what you said about her yesterday," Marty cockily said.

"You a baddie, tell her," said Ronald.

Ignoring those two and one of their many petty arguments, I said, "I panicked at how at ease that person was in my apartment.

When I saw him go into my bathroom and my kitchen, I freaked out." But the creepiest part was him just standing there watching me sleep."

"Now, why would anybody want to watch you sleep? Have you seen you sleeping?" asked Marty.

"For the last time, Marty, shut- the- hell- up!" ordered Ronald.

"I'm just saying. That ain't nothing pretty. You know how Vikki looks when she sleeps. Remember, you said she looks like a…"

"You're this close, Marty," Ronald said, cutting Marty off and holding his thumb and index fingers close together.

"You don't scare me," Marty said just above a whisper.

"I am turning into an emotional cripple."

"Honey, you have every right to be afraid. Especially since you don't know who it is," comforted Ronald.

"Girl, anybody can walk up to you slice your throat, and you won't even see it coming, cause you don't know who to look out for," said Marty.

"Thanks, Marty, that was helpful."

"If you can't say anything constructive, go make some tea," Ronald strongly suggested.

"You gone stop bossing me around. You my lover, not my daddy," Marty said as he got up and walked to the kitchen.

"Sweetie, you keep calling it a 'he.' How do you know it is not a, she?

"I don't know. I guess I used 'he' because 'he' is universal, and women rarely did things like this. If a woman wanted me dead, I'd be dead."

"You said you had a dream. Do you remember it?" asked Ronald.

"It was about my grandmother, who has been dead for over a decade. She wanted me to remember something, some argument. And, she said, do not trust some man."

"Damn! Show us the computer, honey," Ronald asked, shaking his head. We all watched as the hooded stranger walked through my apartment with confidence. Ronald was right; if I knew who it was, I would know what kind of person I was dealing with.

Was he a psychopath? A sociopath? Was he someone I knew: a friend, a coworker, a jilted lover, a relative? The prospects were endless at that point.

After witnessing the hooded person do a walk-through of my condo, and taking a juice out of my refrigerator, then disappearing, Marty asked, "Where did he go? It's like he just disappeared. That's some Houdini shit, right there."

"I know, right. I think something is wrong with the camera system."

Ronald said, "We are not leaving you alone tonight, honey."

That night, Ronald and Marty slept in my living room, and I slept in my bedroom, soundly, peacefully. But to appease my nerves, I put a chair behind the living room door-added security and all.

CHAPTER 47

The next day, Marcus walked around the parking lot, looking for something…anything. There was no trace of anyone having been in the parking lot.

'Vikki said the lights went out one by one, he thought. That was the weather knocking out the power lines and not some horror movie scenario. Last night the weather *was* féroce.'

It had rained heavily, so there should be footprints. Marcus searched the area near and around where my car was parked, and there were no footprints, but the grass appeared trampled.

There was a gum wrapper. Marcus left it there for Detective Conway to see. Marcus placed a call to Detective Conway. Then he went back into the office to wait on the detective.

While seated in his office, Marcus began to think of who might be doing this to me. He also thought of Charlotte.

Avery walked in as Marcus was heavily thinking. Avery was a mentally challenged individual. Despite his deficiencies, he was a very good printer and came highly recommended, so I had hired him.

The other employees would tease him about the way he would stop whatever he was doing when I passed by so he could watch me walk. I got one hell of a sashay.

It was obvious he felt some kind of way about Marcus. I had seen the way he looked at Marcus when he thought no one was looking at him.

Did he suspect something was going on with Marcus and me? Was he jealous? Could he be the perpetrator?

Avery was holding a letter. He told Marcus it was for me, but my door was locked. Everyone knew Marcus, Ronald, and Marty each had spare keys to my office. Marcus told Avery to leave it with him, and he would see to it that I got it.

Avery insisted on leaving the letter in my office. Marcus said, "She's not in, leave it with me, and I will make sure she gets it."

Avery left the letter with Marcus, but not before telling Marcus not to open it, that it was for my eyes only. I think Marcus knew Avery had a little crush on me.

CHAPTER 48

Detective Conway had joined NOPD at age twenty. By the time my *thing* was going on, he had made twenty-seven. He had been on the force for only seven years and had been a highly decorated detective for four of those years.

It was almost unheard of for any officer to become a detective in as few as three years. He was an inspiring young man that took his job very seriously. He was tall, light-skinned, clean-cut, and extremely handsome.

When he walked into the office, the younger females began fixing their hair, checking their makeup, rustling with their clothes, and whispering to one another as he passed them.

Marcus stepped out of his office to greet Detective Conway, looking back at the horny, lusting young women and shaking his head as he closed the door behind them.

"How long have you been seeing Ms. Thompson?"

"Okay, that is how we are going to start the conversation, huh? How did you know something was going on?"

"I'm a detective. I detect things."

"There was, but it is over now."

"Does your wife know?"

"How did you...never mind. Charlotte had her suspicions, but I convinced her that nothing was going on."

"She knows, then."

"Yes."

"Do you think it could be your wife?"

"I thought about it, but I was on the phone with my wife at the time Vikki said she saw a hooded man or woman in the parking lot. I could hear one of my daughters in the background, asking for a glass of water."

"Show me the area in the parking lot you spoke of," said Conway.

As Detective Conway and Marcus were walking to the parking lot, my receptionists, Sidney, said, "God, I hope he is gay. " Monique, my intern, asked, "Why would you want him to be gay?"

"Cause that would explain why he did not notice these puppies," Sidney said, pointing at her boobs.

"Monique replied, "Maybe he is happily married, and his wife has better puppies than yours."

Marcus overheard the conversation between Sidney and Monique. He quickly ushered Conway outside while silently hoping that Conway had not heard the banter.

"How long have you known Ms. Thompson?" Conway asked as they walked outside to examine the parking lot.

"Roughly eight months," said Marcus.

Conway asked if Marcus thought it might have been a disgruntled employee.

Marcus told him that, to his knowledge, everyone was very happy working at my agency. No one had ever complained or been fired.

"The weather was fierce last night, and it would have washed away any footprints the perp may have made, but there patches of grass that appear to have been disturbed," said Conway.

"I said the same thing. Maybe I should become a detective? I could be a black Sherlot Holmes." said Marcus.

"Watch a lot of television, huh?" asked Conway.

"Are you being sarcastic?

"Yep."

They walked to the rear of the parking lot where my car was parked, and Marcus showed the detective the gum wrapper.

Conway put on a glove and put the gum wrapper inside another glove. Then he put the gloves in his pocket. Conway walked around the area where my car was parked, looking for clues.

"Do you think there may be a fingerprint on the gum wrapper?" asked Marcus.

"I'll take it to the lab, and I will know in a few days."

"Good, hopefully, we will finally find out who is doing this to Vikki. It pains me to see her in such a state," said Marcus.

"Got feelings for her, huh?"

"I'm in love with her. She's some kind of special."

"That's not gonna go well for you when your wife finds out."

"I know."

"Let me know when you plan on telling your wife about Vikki so I can reserve a bed for her."

"Really, dude!"

CHAPTER 49

I decided to take a few self-defense classes. I could not depend on Marcus, Ronald, and Marty to always come to my rescue. I needed to learn to rescue myself.

I meant to say, I thought about taking self-defense classes. I had a gun, which was all the self-defense I needed if I could get to it in time.

Detective Conway had suggested I get a dog. I thought since Mark's faulty equipment did not alert me that there was an intruder in my home, getting a dog was the next practical step.

It would be nice to come home to something warm instead of an empty apartment at night. Something that would not judge me and that would love me unconditionally.

Of course, I wanted Joni to help me pick out a dog. When I told Ronald and Marty that I was getting a dog and that Joni was coming with me, Ronald and Marty insisted on coming. Mainly because of the competition thing they got going on with Joni.

The owner of the pet store was shaking her head at the childish display Marty and Joni were putting on. Neither of them was looking at the dogs.

I thought of a Cocker Spaniel or a Labrador, but they were not aggressive enough for me. I needed my dogs to bark loudly.

My choice was two Pomeranian's. A male and a female. I chose Pomeranians because they are fearless, intelligent, playful, and extremely vocal.

And, because they have the tenacity of dogs much larger than they are. I named them Morgan and Freeman. Morgan was my daughter, and Freeman was my son.

As Ronald and I were talking to one of the associates about the Pomeranians, I could hear Joni and Marty still going at it. They had been arguing over what kind of dog I should have.

Joni said I should get a protector, and Marty said I should get something cuddly to come home to since I did not have a man. When Marty went to pick Freeman up, Freeman growled at him. I loved my dogs already.

We went through the store buying bedding, food, collars, and doggie chew toys and a large cage to keep them in when I am not at home. That was to keep them from chewing on my furniture, shoes, and possibly Marty.

After we left the pet store, I made up an excuse to stop at the pharmacy to pick up a pregnancy test. I bought a few other items as well, so none of them would question me. All I needed was for Marty's prying ass looking in my bag and finding a pregnancy test.

First, he would give me that stupid look while planting one hand on his chest. Then the questions would come pouring out like an inquisitive five-year-old.

Well, we brought my children home. Morgan walked through my

apartment, mentally marking her territory by sniffing her surroundings. Freeman went into the kitchen. I guess he was telling me it was time to eat.

Joni sat down on the sofa, and Morgan curled up next to her.

"Awe, I think she likes me," Joni said.

"Bitch ain't got no taste," said Marty.

"Put your face in this, your queerness!" Joni replied, waving her hand side-to-side as though she were fanning away a fly.

Laughing at what Joni had said and the gesture, Ronald said, "I'm going to feed the babies. Marty help Vikki clear us some space for the cage?"

"Oh! So, I'm the help now?" asked Marty.

"You've always been, *the help*," I said.

Marty sucked his teeth and walked over to the box with the cage in it and stood there. He walked from side to side, with one hand on his chin. I guess he was trying to figure out where to start.

Ronald went into the kitchen to prepare meals for my little ones. Morgan had hopped down from Joni's lap and made her way to the kitchen.

After Marty and I finished setting up the cage, I told my guest I was going to take a shower.

So, I said. I wanted to take the pregnancy test, but as I was about to open the package, I read it works best first thing in the morning.

Through the corner of my eye, I could see something scribbled on my mirror. The words *"requiescat in pace,"* which is Latin for "rest in peace," was written in red. And the bastard used my Estes Lauder lipstick.

Marcus always said I had sexy lips, so I complimented them with red lipstick. That bastard had been in my home again.

"How did he get in? I had the locks changed?"

This time I did not want my avenging angels to know the bad guy or guys had been in my apartment again. I would never get rid of them.

I wiped the lipstick off the mirror and told Joni, Ronald, and Marty I was tired and wanted to lie down. As they were leaving Freeman, growled at Marty again.

"I would call you a bitch, but you don't have the necessary parts," said Marty as he walked out. Freeman growled again, only that time he added more bass to his growl.

CHAPTER 50

After everyone had left, I called Marcus. I'm sorry, Charlotte, I thought, but no one is threatening to kill you. I need your husband. I need his strength. I need his comfort.

This whole thing had me so afraid that I had become emotionally attached to Marcus-which was worse than sleeping with him-and, much harder to let go of.

To make sure this visit would not end in sex, I put on my flannel, all-in-one, footie pajamas. You know, the kind of shit we wear that when a man sees you in, he knows sex is not going to happen.

I needed to talk to Marcus. Not just about my intruder wanting me dead, or the note on my mirror, but also about what had happened the day before while I was in my office.

***Ronald and Marty had just come from shopping and wanted to show off their new attires. When I went to stand, something said, "Sit back down!" I practically fell back in my seat.

My head felt heavy, my stomach was churning, and the room started to spin. They both ran to me and asked what was wrong.

Of course, I did not know at the time what was wrong. But, the smell of whatever cologne Marty was wearing had made me sick.

I jumped up and ran to the bathroom, holding my mouth, hoping nothing came out of it until I reached the toilet. Ronald and Marty followed behind me.

I burst through the restroom door, knocking down the plaque that said, 'Wash your hands before you leave this room,' and leaned over the toilet.

It seemed like I would never stop vomiting. Ronald held my hair and gave me comforting words. While Marty, of course, had something shrewd to say.

"Lord, please don't tell me this child is pregnant," he said, throwing his hands in the air.

"Pregnant! I can't be pregnant."

"You had sex, didn't you? Did he wear a condom? Did you wear a condom?" Marty asked.

Once again, Ronald snapped at Marty. "Leave her alone! She is not pregnant; she is catching the flu that's going around."

"Flu–my–ass Marty said, stumping his foot three times! That regurgitating heifer is pregnant. Look at her face. It looks swollen. And her boobies are bigger too."

I looked down at my breasts and realized they had gotten bigger. And my clothes were fitting a little more tightly. I even had to purchase larger underwear. I thought I was just gaining a few pounds and needed more gym time.

Loving a Married Man

First, I had lost a few pounds, but then the weight had come back two-fold. Lord, what if I am pregnant? I thought. How could I have let that happen?

The torrent of thoughts that ran through my head at that moment was so conflicting. On the one hand, it seemed like a good thing, but on the other hand, it was a very bad thing. I had always wanted a baby, but not by someone's husband.

"Honey, if you are pregnant, I know because your biological clock is ticking, you may think of keeping the baby; just remember, it is by a married man," said Ronald.

"Her biological clock has been ticking. Now the alarm is going off," said Marty.

I had to decide—if I was pregnant—whether to keep the baby or not. *Dear God, I want a baby, but with a man of my own. But what if I never got a man of my own? That's was a possibility I had to face. I would never have any children. I would never know the joy of creating another living, breathing, human being inside of me. This pregnancy may well be my only chance to have a child of my own.* I was so fucked!

One of my employees came out of one of the stalls, fastening her pants. When she saw Ronald and Marty in the ladies' room, she turned away from them—not wanting them to see her girlie parts.

"Get over yourself, missy. You ain't got nothing I want to see anyway," said Marty.

Not knowing if she had overheard some of the conversations or not, we all fell silent until she left the restroom.

She noticed I was on the floor next to the toilet and gave me a peculiar look—the kind of look gossip is made of.

She was headed for the door without washing her hands when Marty picked up the sign, that I had knocked down, and blocked her exit.

He put it in her face and asked, "Can you read?" She sucked her teeth as she pushed him aside and walked out the door, but still did not wash her hands.

"That's just nasty. I won't be eating anything from her kitchen," said Marty.

"Honey, if you are pregnant, what are you going to do?" asked Ronald.

"The abortion clinic is open till nine," said Marty.

"Sweetie, I can't say I know how you feel, but whatever you decide, we're here for you," said Ronald.

"I ain't here for her. She let herself get pregnant by a married man. Do you know how that makes me look? I live vicariously through her life," said Marty.

"It is not about you, Marty," said Ronald.

Marcus came into the bathroom to check on me after hearing the other employees gossiping.

"Feeling a bit malade, love?" Marcus asked.

The other employee could not have mentioned that she overheard I was pregnant, or the expression on Marcus' face would have been much different from the one he was wearing.

Noticing me sitting on the side of the toilet, Marcus asked, "What's going on?"

"Look what you did!" shouted Marty as Ronald hurriedly escorted him out of the restroom.

"What?" asked Marcus.

"Like you don't know," said Marty.

"What-the-hell is he going on about?" asked Marcus.

"Nothing...help me up."

Marcus reached out a hand to me. He pulled me up as if I were light as a feather. I walked over to the sink to rinse my mouth out. Marcus followed me. He sat on the side of the sink, holding my hair so it would not get wet.

Marcus asked again what Marty meant by what he had said, and I gave him a vague and bullshit answer. To be honest, I don't know what the hell I said to him. Whatever I said, it was enough for him.***

CHAPTER 51

I thought of sleeping with Marcus to relieve some of the tension I was in. Nothing relieves tension better than sex. I knew I would not be able to sleep, thinking of my death and all the consequences and possibilities of having Marcus's child.

My judgment day had surfaced. My mother would not accept my situation, being pregnant for a married man, since she had stressed so extensively Joni and me staying away from married men, so to her, I would lie.

Deep down inside, I know my mother would not cast away my baby for my mistake. Still, I couldn't subject my son or daughter to a possible rejection from my mother because of what I had done.

I would tell her that I wanted a baby. I wanted to be a mother, but I could not find a man that I was comfortable with. So, I had myself artificially inseminated. Yes, I would lie to my dear mother.

That way, I knew she would accept my baby with no further questions. She would still be upset with me for bringing a child into this world without *a* husband, but it was better than telling her I was bringing a child into this world by *someone else's* husband.

CHAPTER 52

Ronald and Marty could not let yesterday go. It was six-thirty in the evening, and they were banging on my door as if I owed them money. Of course, I let them in, and it began all over again.

"Girl, what the hell you got on?" asked Marty as he strode in.

Ronald began by saying he wanted to give me some time to process things before he came to talk it over with me.

Then he said he could not understand for love, nor money, why women allowed this to happen to them, and Marty saying if they kept their legs closed, it wouldn't happen.

"Why is it that the woman always gets the blame?" I asked.

"Because it is the woman's body that has to go through all the changes. It is the woman that will most likely be raising that child by herself. Why would you do that to yourself, honey?" asked Ronald.

"Ever heard of condoms or birth control pills? Who I'm gone drink with now that you are pregnant? It ain't no fun drinking alone with Ronald," said Marty.

"Heeey…Ronald said, giving Marty an angry look. Hon, be grateful it is just a baby. It could have been something much worse. Condoms are not just to keep you from getting pregnant; they protect you from diseases that could kill you," said Ronald.

"You don't think I know that?"

"Says the woman who hopped in bed with a man and did not demand he wears a condom," blurted Marty.

Do you think he will want the baby, knowing it could ruin his marriage?" asked Ronald

"Girl, he ain't leaving all that money. I heard Marcus' wife is set," said Marty.

"I didn't plan this; it just happened."

"It did not just happen. You had sex education in high school. You knew the risk, and you did it, anyway, said Marty scolding me like a child.

I told them that Marcus is leaving for Manchester in a few months, so he never has to know.

"Now, that's not fair to the child," said Ronald.

"I can't let anyone know Marcus is the father of my baby."

"Girl, you got somebody trying to kill you, and you pregnant by a married man—you fucked ten ways from Sunday! Not six, ten!" said Marty.

Ronald stood up and turned to Marty walking to him slowly. He was shaking his head, trying to understand how someone as smart as Marty was can say the dumbest things.

He put both hands on his hips, looked into Marty's eyes and said, "Your narcissism is not genetic, I know your mother. So, where does it come from?"

Ronald asked, giving Marty an index finger to the forehead.

"Oh, so it's *my* character you want to assault right now, huh? She the one pregnant for a married man," said Marty pointing at me and stumping his feet again.

Ronald bowed his head, let out a deep sigh of surrender, and turned his attention back to me. "Honey, you gotta tell him," he said.

"No way!"

I swore, and I made them swear that we would take this secret to our graves. Only Joni, Ronald, and Marty would ever know. And I would tell Joni when I knew for sure that I was pregnant. First thing in the morning, I would know for sure.

CHAPTER 53

Then there was another knock on the door. I'd almost forgotten I had asked Marcus to come over. I had been planning to tell him that I might be pregnant.

But then I changed my mind after talking with Ronald. I felt ashamed of how careless I had been and that an innocent child was the result of my negligence.

When he saw me dressed the way I was, he smiled. "You mean I'm not getting any more, huh? That getup has 'no sex' written all over it."

"Smart man," I answered.

Then he thought I wanted to talk about my predator. He asked if something else had happened. I showed him the video, and he was as shocked as Ronald, Marty, and I had been.

"Ma Chérie, he was watching you sleep. If he wanted you dead, that would have been the time to do it," said Marcus.

"No shit, Sherlock!" said Marty.

"Did you call the detective?" Marcus asked.

"Not yet."

"Why not yet?"

"I intend to."

"When?"

"Now!"

"Good."

I also told Marcus I had come down with a touch of the flu, which was meant to explain my vomiting before he asked. I was sure he was curious.

Then I told him I needed Ronald, Marty, and him to run things in my absence while I nursed my flu. And, because of everything that had happened, I needed to take a leave of absence for a while.

"Chérie, I don't think being alone right now is a good idea," said Marcus.

"That's what I told her, but she don't listen to nobody," said Marty. Good thing she got them dogs.

Morgan and Freeman had been napping on my bed for hours. It wasn't like them to sleep, so long. It wasn't until they heard Marcus' voice that they woke up. They were scratching at my door for me to let them out.

I introduced Marcus to my extended family members. I told him I got them for added protection. And I had my Glock twenty-six 9mm, so I was good.

"That ain't all she got," said Marty.

"Shush!" demanded Ronald, slightly shoving Marty and then smiling at Marcus.

Marcus looked at Marty curiously then asked how long I would be out. I told him a couple of months, but it might take a bit longer. I honestly did not plan on going back until Marcus was gone.

"A couple of months or longer for the flu?" Marcus asked.

"Not just the flu. With everything that is going on, I have become unglued. I need time to put myself back together again." Okay, my ability to lie, on my feet, had gotten kind of good, huh?

Morgan went over to Marcus and cuddled up next to him, which made Marty furious and jealous.

"Look at that bitch. Like mother, like daughter," said Marty.

Marcus sat down on the sofa, and my Lil ones sat down next to him. Morgan was on his left side, and Freeman sat on his lap.

Marty was standing beside the refrigerator, mocking Marcus as he played with my dogs. I happened to look up and saw Marty making those silly faces at Marcus. I signaled him to cut it out, but that was Marty being Marty.

Then I placed the call to Detective Conway.

CHAPTER 54

While Detective Conway was watching the tape, he asked, "And, your system did not alert you?"

"No," I answered.

"And you don't recognize this person at all?"

"No, I don't."

"At all?"

"No! I said, with more bass in my voice. Well, there is something familiar about him, but I can't put my finger on it.

Detective Conway asked if he could take the tape with him to headquarters to go over it for clues and make copies. Of course, I agreed.

Then Marty started in again and said, "You know, Detective, she gone be in this big-ass condo all by herself, cause she don't want nobody with her."

"You really should have someone with you at all times, you know," Conway stated.

"That's what I told her. She don't listen. She more stubborn than a mule," said Marty.

"I have two dogs, a computerized alarm system, and I have my Glock that I keep with me at all times, so I'm good."

"Those things are fine and dandy, but they won't scare off your stalker, like having people around you would."

"I don't want this person to think that I am so afraid that I am going to crawl into a shell and hideout. Or, let fear consume me to the point of agoraphobia."

"Are you afraid?" Conway asked.

"Hell, yeah!"

"Good; that will keep you on your toes. And a good choice of dogs. They have excellent lungs. You just got train them to bark when someone comes in that door. I'll see you next week with your tape."

"Thanks, detective."

"Please, call me Johann."

"Thanks, Johann."

When I turned from seeing Johann out, Marcus had a jealous look on his face, and Marty was making funny gestures behind Marcus' back.

"Johann, huh?" Marcus said as he walked slowly toward the door to leave. Marty could not resist the temptation to let Marcus know that he knew Marcus was showing a bit of jealousy.

"Ain't that nothing—Mr. Married Man—wanna pee in two spots. Don't you got a wife?" Marty asked.

Marcus turned and looked at Marty with such fury; Marty had to take two steps backward. He took a boxing stance, and said, "I gave you a reason, huh?"

"That's enough, Marty," I yelled.

"Why are you yelling at me? He the one looked like he wanted to do something," stressed Marty.

"You asked for it," I said.

"You ain't in no position to be pissing me off, *MOTHER!*" said Marty.

"What does that plonker mean by that?" Marcus asked in a frustrated tone.

"Nothing, I will call you tomorrow."

After closing the door behind Marcus, I looked at Marty and wanted to wrestle him to the ground, but if I was pregnant, I did not want to damage my baby. I only wanted to damage Marty, so instead, I called him a Bitch!"

He said, "Tramp."

I said, "Slut."

"Harlot."

"Hussy."

"Ho."

"Homo."

"Pregnant by a married man."

"Okay, you win."

CHAPTER 55

When I woke the next morning, I rushed to the bathroom to pee on the little white stick. The instructions said I had to wait for five minutes. That was the longest five minutes of my life.

I went into the kitchen to make a cup of tea while waiting for my destiny to reveal itself. I set my egg timer for five minutes.

After the five minutes were up, I went into the bathroom to read the stick. I took a deep breath before reading it. Two lines, damn!

There I was pregnant, no husband, and someone wanted me dead. My life had taken a turn for the worse. My life seemed like it was traveling through a dark tunnel with no light in sight.

I did not know how Marcus would react to my being pregnant. Would he express joy, or would he be furious because we were careless? Yeah, I said it. *"WE"* were careless! I'm not taking all the blame.

Loving a Married Man

As much as it pained me, I wanted yesterday to be the last time I saw Marcus. I couldn't have him asking me why my clothes were fitting me more tightly, why my breasts had gotten larger, or why I was eating so much more.

This unplanned pregnancy was all my fault. Marcus' beauty blindsided me. I fed off his charm. I should have asked questions. I should have had him investigated. I should have gotten a feeling or something. I should have…

Seeing him standing there yesterday had brought back so many sweet memories. Memories I had to store in the cache of my mind. Precious memories, I could not allow myself to think of any longer.

I know the old saying: "You can't help who you fall in love with," but there is also another old saying: "You can't find happiness from someone else's pain."

I started to feel tense all over again. This moment was no longer a tea moment; it had become a wine moment. Two glasses!

After chucking down my second glass of wine, I called Ronald and Marty to let them know that I wanted to have a meeting this morning at 11:0: clock sharp.

Their instructions were to email all of my staff, including Marcus, and let them know this meeting was mandatory. I wanted to make things clear as to what areas needed attention in my absence and who was in charge.

Then I took a shower and laid down again. I could hear Morgan and Freeman scratching at the door whining. They do that when it is time to go potty.

When I got back from walking them I did not think I would have been able to sleep, but after I laid down I began to drift off. Then, I could feel something cold on the side of my face. Then I heard a click…

Presque la fin...
(Almost the end...)
"la vérité est révélée."
(The truth will be revealed)

CHAPTER 56

"Scream and that sound will be the last sound you hear," the female unsub pressing the cold thing against my face said.

I realized that the cold thing she was pressing against my face was a gun. She yelled at the shadowy figure, who stood silently in the background, and appeared to be a man. "INJECT HER NOW!" she yelled.

The shadowy figure rushed to the side of my bed and grabbed my arm. Even though I knew it was useless to struggle, my sista instincts to survive took over.

I kicked the shadowy person in the chest, knocking him backward onto the floor. The female dropped her guard and got a jab in the nose from my elbow.

Then I felt a pain on the side of my face. That bitch had hit me with the butt of that gun. 'That's gonna leave a bruise,' I thought.

Trying to overthrow my two captures did not go very well. They both managed to pin me down on the bed and inject me anyway. I could feel the needle piercing my skin and the liquid traveling through my veins.

I ended up with a knot on the side of my head and a colossal headache. I was beginning to feel woozy. The male that had injected me also tied my hands and feet. Then he put tape over my mouth.

The female standing over me, holding the gun, was the one that was obviously in charge. The female ordered the male to help her lift me into a large, rolling hamper. As the female placed the gun on the dresser to put me in the hamper I said, "That's my gun!"

As woozy as I was, I thought of my two little wet-nosed bodyguards and wondered why they did not come to my rescue. Or, at the very least, bark to let me know someone was coming in our home.

I spent weeks training those two Lil shits to bark when someone opened the door. They had gotten so good at barking that I slept for more than an hour at a time.

As my predators headed toward my door, I could see my Lil ones asleep in their doggy beds. I bought those Lil bastards as my first line of defense. What were they doing while I am being kidnapped? *Sleeping!*

My sensors did not go off, my dogs did not wake me up, and if that was not bad enough, this crazy woman is kidnapping me with my own shit. That bitch is lucky she got to my gun before I did.

Then I could hear my door open and close. My predators headed towards the service elevator on the opposite side of my floor. Then they stopped dead in their tracks. Through the hamper, I could see Alaina.

Alaina, the-maid-for-hire, was on staff for the tenants that wanted their apartments cleaned. For those of us that had demanding careers and did not have time to clean, Alaina was a godsend.

She was a nineteen-year-old college sophomore majoring in overseas business. At first glance, you would never believe Alaina has an IQ of 132. Mrs. Dayton also a retired business owner would quiz Alaina just to keep her on her toes.

After cleaning Mrs. Dayton's apartment, Alaina was locking the door behind her as my assailants were pushing me out of mime. She walked over to the tenant elevator with her headphones on, semi-dancing, and looking into her cell phone, scrolling her phone with her thumb.

She told me once that her mother had told her she would get run over by a truck, bleeding profusely, and she would still have her nose in her cell phone.

This time having her nose in her phone may have saved her life. Alaina, like most people with cell phones, never bothered to look up.

Their hesitance to move had me wondering that maybe they thought Alaina would turn their way and would recognize them. Or alert the authorities of suspicious activity in our building.

They stood categorically still. And I did not hear either of my assailants so much as breathe. I thought of making a noise or something to alert Alaina of their presence, but I feared if Alaina turned in their direction, she would also become a victim.

Luckily for her, she only heard music. I watched as Alaina walked into the elevator, never knowing that she was that close to a kidnapping or possibly her very own demise. I was relieved. I was falling asleep when one of my captors put tape over my eyes.

CHAPTER 57

Monique was dreaming; she could see Vikki lying on a table. Her hands and feet were strapped to the table, and she had tape over her eyes and mouth. Vikki was terrified. She could feel Vikk's fear.

Monique had fallen asleep on the couch reading *High School with Britt 'N' Gabby*. She liked that book because it reminded her of a time when she was in ninth grade, and she had gotten even with Tina, her bully.

Tina had bullied Monique for months until Monique put green food coloring in her shampoo and body wash bottles. Monique got the idea from the book, *High School with Britt 'N' Gabby*.

Tina screamed so loud they heard her cries over all the sounds of the boys and girls that were still practicing basketball or just goofing around until the bell rang.

A mass of students ran into the locker room to see who was screaming. They all stared at the girl with green hair and hands and a soaked green towel wrapped around her. That moment was priceless to Monique.

Monique realized how good Gabby and Yoni must have felt when they put green food coloring in Mona's shampoo bottle. And just like Gabby and Yoni in the book, Monique had left the building.

When Monique was nine years old, her cousin, Randy, dared her to jump off the roof of her home into her pool. Monique accepted his dare, being the little daredevil that she was.

She had never jumped into the pool from that height before, so the challenge was exciting to her until she hit the water. It seemed like she had landed, headfirst, on the ground from a thousand feet in the air.

Suffering from a few broken bones and a serious concussion, Monique was in a coma for nearly a month. About two weeks later, after being released from the hospital, she had her first premonition.

Monique dreamed her best friend Kizzy would get hit by a car. Thinking it was just a dream, Monique kept her dream to herself. Not less than a week later, Kizzy was hit by a drunk driver.

Monique and Kizzy were playing jacks in Kizzy's driveway when a drunk driver swerved off the street onto the sidewalk. The car hit Kizzy, sending her flying into her mailbox.

Then Kizzy and the mailbox went flying onto her father's car. Not understanding what was happening to her, Monique still did not tell anyone about what she had dreamed.

On a Friday night, Monique dreamed of her teacher, Ms. Dobson. Ms. Dobson was at the hospital. She was sitting on a hospital bed, looking sad and crying.

Someone was lying on the bed with their eyes closed. Others were standing around that person in the hospital bed, and they too were sad and crying.

On Monday morning Ms. Dobson was not in class. The principal, Mr. Atkins, came to inform the students that Ms. Dobson's mother had passed away on Friday night.

At another time, Monique dreamed their neighbors, the Chung's, four houses down, had come into a lot of money and were moving. They had won the lottery.

Over the years, Monique tried to convince herself that her visions and dreams were not real, even though she knew they were. She did not want the people that knew her to call her a witch or bruja by the 28% populace of Hispanics.

That is until Monique dreamed her parents were lying on a Bank's floor bleeding. Monique's parents had gone to the bank to check on some discrepancies in their bank account. There was a bank robbery. Things got out of hand between the bank robber and the swat team.

The bank robber killed everyone in the bank before turning the gun on himself. Monique blamed herself for not warning her parents. To this day, she still regrets not pleading with them to stay at home.

Would they even believe her? Probably not, but at least she would have kept them home long enough for the robbery to happen where her parents would miss the whole thing, or so she thought.

Monique was sent to live with her mother's baby and only brother, Jeremy. Jeremy did not know of Monique's abilities, and Monique was hesitant about telling him.

She did not know if he would accept her or be afraid of her and send her away, and she would be alone again.

***One morning, Monique was tossing and turning dreaming that at 8:15 AM, there was a fifteen-car pile-up on Behrman Highway, and several people were transported to the hospital with serious injuries.

Other injured people sat on the side of the road, bruised and bleeding, being attended to by EMTs (Emergency Medical Technicians.)

Four people did not need transporting to the hospital, nor did they need assistance from the EMTs. Jeremy was one of the four people that lay in the streets covered in cadaver pouches.***

Jeremy had prided himself on never being late and never missing a day of work in ten years. His neighbors would tease him about setting their watches when he would leave his house.

Jeremy would leave his house at exactly 8:0: clock AM every morning. On the way, he would stop at Ariel's bakery and coffee shop to pick up a doughnut and a cup of coffee.

That morning Jeremy would not stop at Ariel's. He would not get a cup of coffee. He would not get a doughnut. He would be late. He did not know it, but being late would save his life.

Monique knew if her uncle Jeremy left at exactly 8:0: clock AM that he would not return. She had to think fast.

Monique thought of a headache but then sacked that thought. Jeremy would only give her aspirin and tell her to lie down. That would not take up enough time to make him late for Behrman Highway.

Jeremy had experienced several times when Monique's menstrual cramps had her in bed all day. Being a man, he was clueless as to how to comfort her, and he would feel bad for her. *'That's it!'* Monique thought. Menstrual cramps it is.

She would tell him that she was in unbearable pain and that she had no more Midol's. She would lie in bed with her fake cramps, her fake moaning, and her fake tears.

Monique knew that Jeremy would have to go in the opposite direction from Behrman Highway to the drug store to get the Midol's, and that would make him late for the 8:15 accident.

Usually, at 8:0 clock, Monique would be in the living room, getting together her last-minute papers for school when Jeremy was about to leave for work. This morning she was not.

When Jeremy went into the living room and saw her book-sack but no Monique, he went to her room and knocked on the door. Hearing her fake moans and groans, he eased the door opened.

He saw his niece lying on her side in bed, curled in a knot, with her knees to her chest, faking her pain, and faking her tears. He asked her what was wrong. Monique explained that she was having cramps, and she didn't have anymore Midol's.

Monique begged Jeremy to go to the drug store to pick up Midol's for her. Jeremy was noticeably agitated at the thought of being late for work. His ten-year track record was about to be broken, and he was not happy about it.

Jeremy thought of giving Monique the money and telling her to go to the drug store herself. But after seeing his little niece in so much fake pain, he did not have the heart.

When he returned from the drug store, Monique was sitting on the sofa watching a special report about the cars crashing, the time of the crash, and the number of people that were injured. Jeremy starred at the television in disbelief. "My God, I could have been in that accident. Luckily for me, I had to get your pills," he stated.

Monique looked up at her uncle, wishing she had told him about the accident. Then he would tell others if he believed her, and maybe the tragedy could have been prevented.

But Monique knew no one would believe her until it was too late. Not only that, but when the world found out about her abilities, she would be labeled as a freak by her peers at school.

Scientist would want to study her; the Military would want to use her as a weapon, and parents with missing children would come knocking on her door all the time.

After the special report had gone off, Monique grabbed her book sack and raced towards the door, not wanting to miss her school bus.

Jeremy yelled, "Nique! Aren't you forgetting something?" holding up the drug store bag. "No uncle J., everything will be all right now," Monique said as she walked out of the door, smiling.

Jeremy stood there, holding the bag with the Mydol pills in his hand and had the most peculiar expression on his face. He went into the kitchen to phone his job and let his employer know he would be late. There was a full bottle of Midol sitting on the countertop. Jeremy scratched his head.

Now Monique had dreamed about Vikki. Monique woke in a cold sweat, breathing heavily. *"Help her!"* a male voice in her head cried out. She could hear it clear as day. As Monique matured, she learned not to ignore her dreams, premonitions, or the voices.

She dashed to the phone to check on Vikki. No answer. She got dressed in a hurry, but before she could leave, the phone rang.

CHAPTER 58

When I began to wake up, I was lying down on a cold table, freezing my ass off. I thought if this lunatic bitch did not kill me, this cold ass table will.

Still groggy from whatever they had given me, I tried to move, but I could not. My hands and feet were still tied. I tried to see, but they had put something over my eyes. I tried to scream, but only muffled sounds came out of my mouth.

Is this my demise. My precious Joni will never see me again. My mother will fall deeper into her depressive state. Ronald and Marty would mourn. Would Marcus mourn? After my autopsy revealed my pregnancy. Will he be sad or relieved?

The straps that fastened my hands and feet were cutting off my circulation. I could hear the female unsub telling the male unsub to make sure the straps were tight and secured. Any tighter and the straps would be tearing into my flesh.

I could hear the male unsub saying, in a whisper, that he was going to take care of that other thing now. Even though his voice was but a whisper, I know I had heard it somewhere before.

After the male unsub had left, the female unsub was behind me, whistling a tune I had not heard since I was a little girl. It was a tune my mother used to hum to Joni and me on those vicious rainy nights.

Joni and I could never sleep when the thunder was pounding on everything in the sky, and lightning would light up our bedroom like a spring festival.

Our mother would come into our room and hum that song until we fell asleep. Why was she whistling that particular tune? Is that tune saying something that I am not hearing?

Where am I? It was so cold, and this place smells like its decaying. I couldn't hear any cars passing by or horns blowing. I couldn't feel air coming from anywhere, either.

I could hear water dripping. The female unsub was fiddling with metal objects behind me. Then I could feel her standing over me. She ripped the tape off of my mouth with such force; I think some of my skin was ripped with it.

As she ripped the tape off my eyes, along with my eyebrows, the woman said, "Well, well, well, look who has decided to join the rest of us in the land of the living.

"As soon as your little sister gets here, you will both be singing your final swan songs. She was tracing my face with something metal, pointy, and cold while staying behind me.

"I know you won't remember me, but I remember you. Oh, I remember you two Lil bastards only too well," the female said.

"What do you mean, my Lil sister is coming? Are you kidnapping her too? What do you want with us? Who are you? Why won't you let me see you? And what the fuck did you drug me with you stupid bitch? I'm pregnant!" I demanded answers.

"I gave you a large dose of ketamine. I couldn't have you screaming your kinky Lil head off, now could I. I needed you to be still. So, I made you still. And I know you are pregnant. I saw the pregnancy box in your bathroom.

"Ketamine could harm my baby," said Vikki.

"Don't worry you'll be long dead before it harms the fetus.

If Joni and I were going to die, I at least wanted to see the face of our killer. And I wanted to know why. Her voice sounded familiar, as well. How do I know that voice? Where had I heard it before?

The woman put her face close to mine and said," You will know who I am soon enough. As soon as your sister gets here, I will explain everything." She grabbed my face with two fingers and shoved my face so hard to the side; I felt my neck snap.

When she walked away from me, I could hear fiddling with the radio until she got to the classical music station. Beethoven's *Fur Elise* was playing. I tried to turn to see what she was doing behind me, but I could not turn far enough. Trying to free myself was even more pointless.

CHAPTER 59

Joni had slept late that morning. She was about to take a shower when she realized her home was quiet. Surprisingly quiet. There was no sweet noise.

There was always sweet noise in her home at that time of the morning. Javon and Lovec would be running through the house. Steven would be trying his best to quiet them so Joni could sleep late.

Joni looked at the clock on her bedroom wall. It was 10:15 AM. There were no sounds — not even cartoons playing on the television. Joni went down the hall of their two-story home and checked Jovan's room and then Lovec's. No children. She called out to Steven. No husband.

She went downstairs to the kitchen, and there was a note on the refrigerator door. Steven had taken the children out for the day. He drew several hearts on the note. Inside each heart was the words; I love you. He was romantic like that.

Joni's unwanted guest had visited her the night before. That monthly visitor had always transformed Joni from happy mommy to mean mommy. The first day of the visit was always worse.

Joni was almost impossible to be around. Doors and cabinets were being slammed shut. Things were being tossed around, and she used unfavorable words.

Their peaceful home would become a war zone. After the first day, mean mommy would leave, and happy mommy would return.

To escape the mean mommy, Steven had sneaked the kids out of the house while Joni was still asleep. The note he left Joni said they would be gone most of the day and that she should enjoy the peace.

Elated at having the time to herself, Joni charted out her day. After she showered, she would treat herself to breakfast at Durrell's breakfast bar. Then, she would go to the spa.

She would get aromatherapy, a massage, get her hair and nails done, and she would get her skin exfoliated. She would call Vikki, and they would have lunch. Then she would shop.

Joni dressed quickly. She did not want to waste another second of this precious day. No husband, no kids, it was like being single again.

As she opened the kitchen door that led to the garage, she noticed Steven's car was still in the garage. She walked over to Steven's car and looked in the window. No, Steven, no kids.

As she was about to turn to check her house again for her husband and children, a man was standing there, blocking her way.

Before she could ask who he was, he stuck her in the neck with a needle. Almost immediately, she felt light-headed. She was confused, and her speech became slurred.

Joni began to lose consciousness. She lost her balance, trying to get away and began to fall. The man caught her put her in the passenger side of her car. And then, for Joni, darkness filled the garage. The intruding male opened the garage door and drove off.

The male unsub had one more errand to run. A letter had to be delivered, a very special letter.

CHAPTER 60

Ronald and Marty arrived early to have a two-on-one with me before the meeting. Surprised that I had not made it there, Marty called my cell phone.

Getting no answer, he figured I was on my way. Everyone that knew me knew I would never answer my cell phone while I was driving. Still, it is not like Vikki to not be here early, Marty thought.

Ronald decided to call my landline phone at my apartment to see if maybe I had overslept, being pregnant and all. Still, no answer.

The employees had started to arrive between 10:30 AM to 10:45 AM, but still no Vikki, and two other employees were MIA (Missing in Action) as well, Monique and Avery.

Ronald started to call Avery to remind him of the meeting, but Marty said he was not the most valuable player and that it did not matter if he showed or not. Ronald had to firmly remind Marty that the meeting was mandatory and dialed Avery again. No answer. Then Ronald dialed Monique.

When Ronald called Monique, she answered on the second ring and said, "Can't talk now," and hung up the phone. Ronald looked at the phone, not believing what had just happened and asked, "Did that Lil hooker hang up on me?"

"That's all right, boo, she know we gone get her?" said Marty putting his arm around Ronald as Marcus walked into the room.

Marcus arrived at 11:50 AM, asking for me. Ronald told him I hadn't made it in yet. "That's not like Vikki. Did anyone try to contact her?" asked Marcus.

"Now, there's a thought," Marty said sarcastically.

"I'm going over there. Give me one of your keys?" asked Marcus.

"You ain't getting mine. Vikki don't like nobody snooping around her apartment when she ain't home. Our keys are for emergencies only," said Marty.

"Dude! You blimey arsehole! With everything that is going on. Vikki scheduled a meeting, and she is not here; she is not answering her cell phone! Think you, nutter! She could be in trouble or hurt!" said Marcus.

"Oh My God, I hope they don't hurt the baby. Oh shit! said Marty putting his head down. Realizing he had said too much, Marty tried to avert the subject onto something else. "What the hell is a arsehole?" Marty asked Ronald, turning his back to Marcus.

"What, baby?" asked Marcus.

"What, baby?" Marcus asked again, walking closer to Marty. Marcus grabbed Marty's arm, turning Marty around to face him. "WHAT BABY!?" Marty knew it was useless to try and think of a lie.

Plus, as much as he did not like Marcus and that Marcus was the father of Vikki's baby, that was a secret he was not happy with keeping.

"Vikki is pregnant, and you're the baby daddy," said Ronald.

"What?" asked Marcus

"You heard him," said Marty.

Marcus sat down in Vikki's chair in the conference room. He put his head down with his hands together as if praying. Now he understood why Vikki felt the need to end their relationship.

'Why didn't she tell me? Marcus thought. *Did she think I would not want her or the baby? Did she think I would be angry with her?*

CHAPTER 61

Marcus, Ronald, and Marty arrived at Vikki's apartment at nearly the same time as Monique. When Marcus saw Monique, he asked her what was she doing there? Monique told Marcus that Vikki was not answering her phone, and she got a little nervous because of everything Vikki is going through.

That was not the whole truth. Monique thought that if she was in Vikki's apartment, she might be able to sense her whereabouts and maybe who had taken her.

"Hold on, missy! How were you gone get in? Nobody has a key but Ronald and me, her mom, and that holy-ass sister of hers," said Marty.

"Well, if Vikki did not open her door, I was going to ask Jason, the doorman, to let me in," said Monique.

Ronald walked over to Monique slowly with one hand on his hip, and the other hand was pointing his finger at her.

In a slightly elevated tone, he said, "You hung up on me, I'm gone get you for that, INTERN!"

"I know, said Monique, letting out a deep sigh. The copy machine will be my best friend for the next week."

Marcus opened the door, and to his surprise, there was nothing out of place. He entered, thinking if someone tried to abduct Vikki, she would have put up a fight.

Vikki's purse was still on the dresser, her cell phone was on the charger, her bed was left unmade, and her Glock was missing.

"Where is her gun? Somethings wrong said, Ronald.

"You think!" said Marty. Ms. Prissy don't go nowhere without her cell phone, her makeup."

Monique walked around the living room, trying to sense something. Her feelings were not as strong in the living room. Everything was kind of fuzzy.

Monique went into the kitchen. Still, she felt nothing. The dogs were sleeping peacefully. She wondered how they could sleep through all this ruckus. When she entered Vikki's bedroom, it was like the light in her head came on.

She can see four people: a man, a woman, and Vikki. The fourth person is kind of vague. Vikki struggled with the man and the woman. The man stuck Vikki with a needle. The man and woman put her in a clothes hamper, and they put her in the back of a van.

"What the hell is wrong with you, intern?" asked Marty.

Marcus was on the phone waiting to be patched through to Detective Conway when he also noticed Monique. He had remembered that *thing,* that Monique was doing, being done before, in his home town.

In Manchester, there was a woman that would help the local Bobbies find criminals or missing persons. That lady would do the same thing Monique was doing, walking around touching things. Concentrating...

After Marcus hung up the phone with Detective Conway, he sat back in the chair. He rubbed his chin with his index finger and his thumb, as he watched Monique explore.

Marcus got up from the chair and walked over to Monique and asked, "You're sensitive, aren't you? You can sense things that only a few people like you can.?" "Yes," answered Monique.

"Sense what?" asked Marty.

"Shush! Let her finish," demanded Marcus. Marcus said, "Baby girl, tell us everything you feel and see."

With her eyes closed, Monique said, "After the man and woman took her from here, they put her in the back of a Van. I don't know where they took her; it's like they went off my radar for a few minutes.

I can see Vikki lying on a table. Her hands and feet are tied, she can't move.

She has something over her eyes and mouth. She can't see or scream for help."

"What the hell is going on? How does she know that? Marty asked in a whisper, leaning close to Ronald.

"Shush!" said Ronald.

"Let one more person shush me today. Just one more!" said Marty

"Ignoring what Marty just said Marcus asked, "What else do you see, Monique?"

"It's only two of them. I can't make out their faces, but there is something familiar about the man. I keep seeing a shirt with an emblem of a lion on it."

"What kind of shirt?"

"A white, short-sleeved shirt with a lion on the pocket."

"Oh shit! You one of them soothsayers? You did not see what I did last Saturday night, did you? asked Marty leaning close to Monique. Cause if you did, don't tell Ronald."

"If you and Ronald stop picking on me, my lips will be glued shut. Otherwise, I will tell everything I saw," said Monique.

"Why you, Lil…said Marty as he watched Monique walk away in victory.

Monique did not have a clue as to what Marty was talking about, but he had opened the door to end her workplace drama, and she walked through it.

Monique went to the other side of the bed. She told Marcus that they had taken her from there. The man stuck a needle in her arm and helped the woman put her in a clothes hamper. That's all I'm picking up.

"Are you sure about this baby girl?" asked Marcus.

"No! Sometimes I see things before it happens. Sometimes I see things while it happens, and sometimes I see things after it has happened. Sometimes I am way off track. I keep picking up four people: the man, the woman, Vikki, and someone else.

When I see Vikki, I sense two people. That's how wrong I can sometimes be. Most times, I have to interpret my visions to understand them myself.

"What I can tell you is that Vikki does not have much time left, said Monique. I see four people, and the bad people are waiting for a fifth person.

"When that fifth person comes, it's game over for Vikki and the other two people. And, I keep seeing that white shirt. We have to figure out what that white shirt is trying to tell us before it is too late."

"How do you know it is game over for them?"

"I don't know. I just sense it."

CHAPTER 62

Conway responded with his partner and uncle Damian. Damian had been on administrative leave for beating a man that was beating his wife. A few minutes before the forensics team arrived, Marcus filled Conway and Damian in on what they knew.

Marcus told Conway and Damian that two people had taken, Vikki and that they were keeping her somewhere. He did not know where they had taken her, only that she is tied up. "One more thing said, Marcus. Vikki's pregnant.

"And he the baby daddy," blurted Marty from across the room. Marcus turned to give Marty a not now, but I'm going to kick your ass later, look.

"VIKKI'S PREGNANT? That is why I keep seeing two people when I see Vikki. I thought my antennas were crossed again. It happens sometimes," said Monique.

"I'll need a recent picture of Vikki so I can put an APB (All Points Bulletin) or BOLO (Be On The Look OUT) on her," said Conway. Marcus reached in his back pocket and pulled a picture out of his wallet. It was a picture of him and Vikki on their trip to Biloxi.

"Marcus! Dude! Do you keep a picture of Vikki in your wallet?" asked Conway.

"Yeah, why?"

"Seriously! Brah!," Conway said as he walked off, smiling and shaking his head. Conway spoke into his hand radio to an NOPD dispatcher, putting out an APB on an African American female named Victoria Thompson.

Conway also told the dispatcher he was forwarding a picture of her along with her height, weight, eye, and hair color.

"She pregnant. Don't forget to tell them she pregnant," shouted Marty.

"How far along is she?" asked Conway.

"Oh, we don't know that. Vikki ain't been to the doctor yet," Marty said, walking off.

Conway spoke into his radio again, alerting all available cars that the African American female was pregnant. Conway turned to see Monique standing in Vikki's bedroom door, biting her nails, looking as if she wanted to say something.

Forensics walked into the living room and began to unpack their equipment. Conway turned his gaze from Monique and instructed one member of the forensics team to fingerprint the living room doorknob first.

Monique raised her hand and cleared her throat to get Conway's attention. "I think you should start here, in the bedroom, but you won't find any prints anywhere in this apartment.

"You won't find a trace of them being here. Vikki's assailants were wearing gloves, painters masks, painters coveralls, painters hats, sunshades, and shoe covers."

"And how would you know that, young lady?" asked Conway.

"I see and dream things. Sometimes it is things that had already happened, and sometimes it is things that will happen. And sometimes it is things that are happening now. That's how I know Vikki is still alive," answered Monique.

"So, you're telling me that you are an alchemist."

"Kinda, but I can't see or talk to the dead, but sometimes I can hear them."

"What type of things do you see?"

"Like Vikki was taken from her bedroom, and if we don't do something soon, she is going to die. Her and the baby." And, someone else is coming. Then all three of them are going to die," said Monique.

Conway turned to look at Marcus for some reasoning. Marcus shrugged his shoulders and said, "She's one of *those* people."

Conway said, "Not saying I believe you, but what else did you see?"

"I think it was a man and a woman. I can't see their faces to describe them because they wore disguises."

"How can you tell that it is a male and female if they are wearing disguises?"

"Just like I can tell you are a man and I am a woman. A person's body build gives them away. Also, I keep seeing a white short sleeve shirt, and it looked like it had a picture of a lion on the pocket."

"It sounds like some school or work uniform. Unc, can you check which schools or businesses have a lion on the front pocket. "On it," said Damian.

Marcus began to pace nervously, wondering if he will ever get the chance to tell Vikki that he wanted her and the baby. He went over and stood by the window, trying to hide the tears that were forming in his eyes. Marcus began to pray. Something he had never done.

"Wait a minute, said Marty. Didn't Avery wear a shirt like that once?" he asked, looking at Ronald.

"I believe he did. It was at our Halloween party a few years ago, said Ronald. But Avery don't have the sharps to pull something like this off."

"If it is him, he's not acting alone. What's Avery's full name?" asked Conway.

"We don't know. We don't pay much attention to Avery except when he is starring at Vikki," said Marty

"He stares at Vikki a lot?" asked Conway

"Yeah, and we stare at him a lot. Lately, he has been looking kinda sad when he looks at her like he knows a woman like Vikki will never go for him," said Ronald.

Then Marty leaned closer to Conway and whispered, "he just a copy boy, and he kinda slow. Like he was dropped on his head when he was a baby, and when his mama picked him up, she left his brains on the floor."

Conway, visibly irritated with Marty, had turned to Marcus to ask him to go to Vikki's office and find out Avery's last name. Marcus had gone back into Vikki's bedroom.

He was sitting on Vikki's bed reminiscing of all the times Vikki and he had made love on that bed. All the times they had laughed on that bed. The last time she had cried on that bed.

He wondered if he would ever have those times with her again? He could no longer hold back his tears. He sneaked out while no one was watching.

CHAPTER 63

"**Y**ou honestly don't know who I am, do you?" the female unsub asked Vikki. Well, I remember you and that other youngin. Let's see; it was May of 1982 when I found out that your loosey-goosey mother was sleeping with my husband.

"My husband's name was Michael, in case you did not know. In the first few years of my marriage to Michael, I had two miscarriages.

"The doctors said I could not have any more children. So what was the point of sleeping with Michael? He could not give me a child. We even slept in separate bedrooms.

"At first, I said nothing about your mother sleeping with my husband because I did not mind her fulfilling my duties. You see, my dear men have needs.

"But, years later, when I found out about you two little mongrels, his infidelity had become too much to bear. I wanted to be the one to have my husband's children.

"It was on October 9th when the insurance adjuster called to verify your ages and needed your social security numbers.

That unfaithful bastard of mine was leaving your mother a three-million-dollar insurance policy. And if anything happened to your mother, you two rugrats would get the money.

"There was no way I could stop the insurance policy; believe me, I tried. I tried canceling the policy, and when that did not work, I tried calling the bank to stop the payment. That did not work either. That's when I visited your mother.

"You were a little girl when I first saw you. I was trying to talk some sense into that nappy head of your hers. I warned her. I even offered her money to go away. That silly fool said she loved Michael and would never leave him.

"So, she left me with no choice. Have you figured out who I'm talking about yet? No, not yet. Somewhat slow are ya? I'm talking about your father, your mother's boyfriend, my husband. My husband was your father. Got it now, you Lil mutt.

I remember. There was a man that used to visit my mother when I was little. He used to bring me and Joni things. He used to play with us. He used to tell Joni and me that he loved us more than anything in this world. That man was our father. Why wouldn't our mother tell us about him?"

"The night before your father's unfortunate demise, he was foolish enough to ask me for a divorce. He told me he was in love with your mother and wanted to be a full-time father to his girls.

"I wanted to bash his head in that night, slamming her fist on the table where Vikki lied. I could not let him do that. Leave me, his forbidden fruit, his trophy wife, for some coffee server, some coon.

"The morning after he'd asked me for a divorce, I was standing at my kitchen window admiring my beautiful flower arrangements.

"The purple and blue tulips that lined the back wall hid a special flower I bought specifically for your father. My Aconitum Variegatum, more commonly known as Wolfsbane. The queen of all poisons-the queen of all husband killers.

"This particular flower, when given in small amounts, only sickens you and may cause some gastric discomfort for a while. Eventually, it kills you. The morning after, Michael said he was leaving me for a chain dragger. I knew it was time for the grand finale.

"First, I gathered my pretty little purple flower. Then I grind it into tiny little particles using my pestle and mortar. I put three scoops of Michael's favorite coffee in a Ziploc bag along with my pretty purple flower and shook them well.

"Then I brewed his morning coffee. His coffee was waiting for him when he came out of his study. I also poured myself a cup, just for show.

"Cream and sugar, dear?" I asked.

"Just sugar, he answered. I hope our conversation last night didn't come as a total surprise to you, Mary. Let's face it; we have never been what you would call happy. We don't even sleep in the same bed," said Michael. We both deserve to be happy, don't you think?"

"Yes dear."

"Do you understand and accept the terms of the divorce?" asked Michael.

"Of course, dear."

"The terms were that if I did not contest the divorce, I could have all my personal belongings (jewelry, clothing, etc.). The house with all the interiors and exteriors and both cars would be mine.

"Not to mention, half the bank account, and a sizable allowance each month. All Michael would take with him was his personal belongings.

"Then he drank the coffee, none the wiser. Watching that smirk-ass look on his face, like he had swallowed the proverbial canary, irritated me so much, I wanted to shove that cup down his throat.

"For a brief moment, I was tempted to tell him then that he had drunk my special brew, to scare the shit out of him. But..., my patience would make my reward far more gratifying.

"I could barely hide my smile as he took another sip of my special coffee. I thought of all the times Michael had irritated me when he sipped his coffee. It sounded like a dog slurping from a dog bowl.

"Keep drinking, dear. Finish all of the poisoned coffee for mama. That little adulterous bitch can have your 'COLD-DEAD-BODY."

"Your coffee tastes a little bitter this morning, my dear," your *father* said.

"Maybe the coffee pot needs to be cleaned," I replied.

"Michael had the gall to ask me if I were going to be all right before he turned to look at me and opened the door to leave.

"Like asking me for a divorce was okay, and I would not feel betrayed or abandoned–hopeless or useless–*alone*. Michael thanked me for the coffee and gave me a half-smile before closing the door behind him.

I assumed he was on his way to see your maw so they could discuss their wedding plans. I was hoping that is where he was headed.

"I slid the curtains open just a little, so I could watch him get into his car to go to your mother's apartment. He had a stupid grin on his face. He was whistling–thinking he was about to be happy.

"Not knowing that would be the last time he would whistle, that would be the last time he would be happy.

"I knew it would be about fifteen minutes before Michael started to feel a little queasy from the poison, but, by then, he would have made it to your mother's apartment.

"I wanted her to watch Michael die. I wanted her to feel the pain in her heart as she had caused in mine. I'd wished I could have seen the expression on his face when he knew that, that would be the last time he would see *her* face.

"I wondered how he felt, at that moment, when he realized he would not be around to raise his precious little girls that he was leaving me for.

"Anyway, I'd planned everything perfectly, right down to the clean-up. I put on some Latex rubber gloves.

I filled the sink with water and added half a gallon of bleach and a half-gallon of vinegar to it. I placed the coffee pot, pestle and mortar, and both coffee cups and saucers in the sink.

"I flushed the coffee grinds down the toilet. Then I cut up the latex rubber gloves and Ziploc bag into tiny pieces and flushed them down the toilet.

Then I poured some vinegar and water in the coffee pot and brewed away any trace of poison. Then I brewed plain water to kill the vinegar smell. I even soaked the scissors that I used to cut up my gloves and Ziploc bag.

After I had cleaned everything, I had used that had poison residues like the countertop and table. I went outside and planted another purple tulip where the wolfbane had been planted.

Then, I brewed a regular pot of coffee for myself, minus the poison. All that was left to do was practice my tears of being sad for losing my husband.

October 12, 1987, was the day I made sure that death would divorce your father and me, not a piece of paper. That's right, nigger child. I killed your daddy."

"Oh my god! Today is October 12th. My mind began to pull memories out of

its cache. I remembered that night of the argument; it was also a stormy night. Joni sat in bed with her knees up to her chest-trembling.

"I had wondered why our mother had not come to our aid when she knew how nights like that affected us. I got out of bed to find her. As I walked down the hall, I could hear loud voices.

"I peeked in the living room. I could see my mother arguing with a lady. The lady seemed very upset with my mother. "Remember the argument," my grandmother had said,

"I wish I could see your mother's face when she reads the note my son left on her door."

CHAPTER 64

Marcus had gone back to the office to see if he could find any clues as to Vikki's whereabouts. He noticed the letter Avery had left for Vikki and decided to read it.

The note read: *Dear Ms. Thompson, this is Avery, your printer. I am writing this note to tell you that I am very sorry for doing the things to you that my mother told me to do. I did not want to do those things to you until one day, I was coming to work, and I saw you kissing Marcus. I was watching you from downstairs. I was very mad at you. I gave you those black roses. I was the one that messed up your office. I was the one that threw around the things on your patio. My mother wrote those bad words on your grass, though. My mother and me was the ones that followed you around. I am not proud of what I had done to you. At first, I thought my mother just wanted to scare you. Now I think my mother is going to hurt you and your sister. I like you, and I don't want to scare you anymore. I don't want to hurt you or your sister either. If you and your sister can run away, so my mother won't find you run very fast. This is Avery, your printer saying I am sorry." XOXOXO*

Marcus grabbed the phone and dialed Detective Conway immediately. After reading the letter to Conway, Marcus tried to get in touch with Joni, but her cell phone kept going to voicemail. He tried her landline phone, and it just rang and rang and rang.

Marcus called Conway again. "Joni is not answering her phone," said Marcus. "Joni would be Vikki's little sister, right?" asked Conway. "Yes." Said Marcus "The note said Avery's mother wanted to hurt Vikki and her little sister. The culprits must have the little sister too?"

Conway asked Marcus to look in Avery's file for Avery's address. Marcus rushed to the file cabinet, throwing files on the floor and into the air until he got to Avery's Duncan's file.

As it turned out, Avery's address was across the river in Jefferson Parish, but his emergency contact was his mother, and she lived right next door to Vikki. Her name was Mary Pearson.

"Bloody hell! This whole thing is going all to pots. It looks like Avery and his mother are doing this to Vikki, said Marcus. But why?"

"Does Vikki have any other relatives other than her mother and sister?" Conway asked Marcus. I need to get as much information on Vikki as I can so I can figure out what-the-hell is going on."

"Not that I know of," said Marcus. You can ask Ronald and Marty; they know more about Vikki's family than I do. Have you questioned Vikki's mother yet? She may know something."

"Do you have a number for Vikki's mother?" "No, I don't, but it must be in her cell phone," said Marcus. "What is her name?" "Shirley."

After hanging up with Marcus, Conway went into Vikki's bedroom and seized her phone. "Jesus! Conway said after pulling up Vikki's contacts. How many contacts does this woman have?"

Conway tried M for Mom. There were several M's. The first was Madison's Boutique. Then Majestic cleaners, Maimi Printing Paper, Mason's machine repair, etc., but no mom.

Finally, Conway got to the S's for Shirley. There was Salvation dog grooming, Savory foods, Shillin's pizza delivery, and Stillman's liquor store, etc., but no Shirley.

Frustrated, Conway held Vikki's phoned in the air and asked if anyone knew what name Vikki would list her mother under in her phone. Marty answered and said, "Vikki's mom is under B for 'Beautiful Goddess." "Really? Beautiful Goddess."

CHAPTER 65

Shirley had raised her girls in a well-to-do neighborhood just off Saint Charles Avenue. Being a single parent, she played the role of both mother and father. She was a bit stern and very protective of her girls.

Shirley had been thinking about her girls more than usual that morning. She had tried to call both of them, but neither answered, and she could only leave a message. An uneasy feeling had crept upon her.

However, there had been times when Vikki nor Joni would answer their phone when Shirley would call after they had some argument or another.

Shirley had clung to them like a spider in its web all their lives. They never understood why, and she did not have the heart to tell them. How could she? What would she say?

Vikki and Joni did not know it, but it was them that kept Shirley's memories of a wonderful life, alive. Fond memories she would always cherish.

Shirley had just finished her morning walk, followed by several women's vitamins. Then she would complete her morning ritual with her daily workout.

She would pour herself a cup of coffee, sit on the sofa, and watch several workout videos. Before she could put the tape in the tape recorder, the phone rang.

Everyone that knew Shirley knew that between 11:o clock AM and 12:0 clock PM, she would be working out and not to disturb her. Thinking it was a telemarketer, she was ready to tell the minute consuming vultures to back-the-hell-off.

"Hello, is this Mrs. Thompson?" asked Conway. "Yes, and it is Ms., not Mrs.," said Shirley. "My name is Detective Conway, and I must meet with you. Are you available?" "Yes, what is this about?" "I'd rather discuss this in person. May I swing by?" "Sure."

"What have my girls done now?"

CHAPTER 66

"**S**o you are the person that was arguing with my mother one night when I was a little girl?" I asked.

"Most likely. Unless my husband was not the only married man, your strumpet mother was screwing. I knew someday I would make her pay for her and my husbands' betrayal," said the female unsub.

The female unsub walked in front of me. When I could gather all of my vision, I was shocked to see who my kidnapper was. It was my neighbor, Mrs. Pearson.

I was more baffled than ever. "What could my little sister or I have possibly done to you for you to want us dead?"

"You were born."

I read in a magazine once that in cases like this, it is best to remain calm as not to agitate your assailant and cause the situation to escalate instead of defusing.

But it was too late, to see that it was my neighbor that had taken me from my home and she is the one that wants me dead, made me agitated, and I was ready to escalate the situation.

"Oh, hell, no! Bitch! Untie me, I am going to kick your lily-white ass," I futilely said. Like that was going to make her untie me.

"I'll untie you when I am ready to throw your dead-ass body in the Mississippi River," she replied.

"I understand that you are upset with my mother and your husband, but my sister and I had nothing to do with this. Why do you want to hurt us?" I asked.

"The sins of the mother, child... Exodus 34:7. Your mother had an affair with my husband. Together they conceived two bastard girls. Now, you and that Lil raggedy-ass sister of yours will pay for their sins.

"My husband was going to leave me for that shameless hussy until I stopped him. I made sure he'll never have another affair.

"Because you killed him, you deranged bitch!'

"Yeah, I did, but you know it wasn't bad enough that Michael wanted to leave the marriage, he wanted to leave me for a niggress. Now that was unacceptable. I would have been shunned from all respectable society.

"Then I thought, if he died, while still married to me, I could still have my place in good society." "Is that what this is all about?" I asked.

"No, dumette! Are you listening to me?" Mary asked, giving me a shove against the head.

"I heard you! You are a scorned woman, blah, blah, blah," I said.

"You heard what I said, but I need you to listen. When you hear my words, they go in one ear and out the other, and you forget the importance of what was said. But, when you listen, your tiny little brain will process what I said, and you remember what I said.

"Now, are you listening? Mary asked again, pulling Vikki's hair. I honestly thought all these feelings I have were laid to rest when Michael died until I saw you."

"You looked so much like your father that the rage that I thought I had buried deep in the back of my mind came rushing to the surface. I couldn't control my anger. I couldn't control the desperate need to make you and your sister dead.

"I sometimes watched from across the street as you and your employees moved around that office building. I wanted to blow that fucking building up with you in it.

"My son and I watched you kiss that man that I later found out was married. The apple does not fall from that tree, I see. You were going to ruin that woman's life like your mother had ruined mine.

"If that was not bad enough, before I took you from your apartment, I noticed a pregnancy test box in your bedroom. I dug through the trash in your bathroom and found the stick.

"That was when I decided; this bitch has got to die. But I did not want you to die alone, so I decided it was best if your sister joined you. That way, your harlot of a mother would feel twice the pain.

"I followed you around, learning your ways and habits. I patiently waited for this moment. I wanted you, girls, to die on the same day your father died. Your sister will be joining us soon. Now that's Poetic Justice, don't you think.

"What better way to get my revenge on that bitch-ass mother of yours than to take the life of her two illegitimate lassies. My only wish is that Michael is somewhere watching this.

CHAPTER 67

George and Kevin Robertson were brothers that had started their architectural firm well over fifteen years ago. Conway's mother, Bernice, was their first customer.

Bernice wanted a home built from the ground up. She had hired George and Kevin to draw up the plans for her new home. Conway was a little boy when George and Kevin first met him.

Even as a child, Conway had impressed the two. George and Kevin took Conway to his first strip club for his eighteenth birthday that Bernice never found out about, and several Saints games.

Bernice had invited George and Kevin to Bar-b-ques, birthday parties, and other family functions. They took over the role of clone-father for Conway when his father passed when Conway was only twelve.

So when Conway said he needed blueprints of Vikki's apartment building, they were more than happy to oblige. In return, if they needed a permit for a building in a hurry, Conway would make a call.

George immediately faxed the blueprints to the number in Conway's squad car. Damian was in the squad car at the time the fax came in. Damian hurried upstairs to show Conway what the blueprints revealed.

Conway carefully examined the blueprints and discovered how Avery and his mother had been entering and exiting Vikki's apartment. "I must admit, said Conway. They even had me thinking they were Houdini's."

Conway called Marcus and put him on speakerphone so he could explain to everyone what he had learned. Marcus listened eagerly while cleaning up the mess of papers he made.

He laid the blueprints across the kitchen table. Conway said, "In the 16, 17, and 1800s, Vikki's apartment building used to be a large mansion. In

348

those days most mansions had secret passageways.

The owners of the mansions that did not believe in slavery would hide the slaves until it was safe for the slaves to be transported up North.

"In 1965, when the owners of the house turned the house into apartments, they had to expand on both sides. Vikki's apartment was in the middle and had very few changes made to it.

"As you can see, the closet in Vikki's living room is connected to the closet in the Pearson's apartment. And, it is directly under the camera. That's how they were able to get in and out without being seen coming through the door.

"But how did they not trigger the sensors?" asked Marcus.

"My guess is faulty equipment, said Conway. When this is over, Vikki should ask for a refund. Now that we suspect who may have Vikki, we need to find out why the suspect has Vikki.

"Maybe the "why" will give us a clue as to the "where." I think it's time we have a little chat with Vikki's mother. And by the way, Marcus, we are going to have a little chat about that disappearing act you pulled."

"What about the dogs?" asked Marcus.

"They're asleep. What about the dogs?" asked Conway.

"Detective, they are Pomeranian's, why are they sleeping? They should be barking at the strangers in Vikki's home."

"You're right," said Conway. Conway kneeled and checked the pulse on both dogs to see if they were dead or just sleeping. "They're alive. Poor Lil things they must have been drugged as well."

"My poor BFF. Vikki got useless dogs, a useless security system, a useless gun, and she got pregnant by a useless man," said Marty.

"YOU FUCKING WANKER, I AM GOING TO KICK YOUR BLOODY AMERICAN ARSE WHEN THIS IS OVER!" shouted Marcus.

Marty poked his tongue at the telephone, then looked at Conway and asked, "I did not understand a damn thing he said, did you?"

When Conway grinned and turned to leave, Marty blocked him at the door, leaned in closer, and whispered, "Do me a favor Constable and do not tell Vikki's mother that she is pregnant.

"Vikki's mom is like a real Christian lady, and Vikki said she was gonna lie to her mother about the father cause she don't want her mother to know that she is pregnant by a married man."

"Seriously! That's your worry right now," asked Conway as he briskly closed the door behind him.

"Well, God damn," said Marty taking a step back, putting his hand on his chest after realizing Conway was not interested in hearing what he had to say.

Ronald could hear Marcus mumbling something through the phone and asked him to repeat it. Marcus said that he wanted them to keep him on speakerphone so he could hear what's going on.

"Dude, what if Vikki tries to call?" asked Ronald.

"Unbelievable! Are you barmy? Do you really think that if Vikki gets free, she is going to call her home phone on the off chance that we are all there waiting for her to call?" asked Marcus.

Monique giggled and said, "Good one."

Conway and Damian had gone downstairs to their cruiser to looked up the shortest route to Vikki's mother's house. "There is basic information on Vikki, her mother, and her sister, but no Father," said Conway.

"I'm curious to know who and where their dad is," said Damian.

"So am I, unc, so am I."

CHAPTER 68

As Conway and Damian cruised down Saint Charles Avenue en route to Vikki's mother's house, they passed a Popeye's. "Step on it, unc, time is not on our side," said Conway

Conway watched with pride as his uncle maneuvered the cruiser and remembered that his uncle was the reason he wanted to become a police officer.

When Conway was a teenager, his uncle would come to his mother's house in his uniform. Young Conway was so proud of his uncle.

Conway would ask his uncle Damian to tell him stories about his day as a crime fighter. The stories would be so riveting that Conway could hardly wait until he was twenty so he could join the force.

Conway remembered the first time, as a rookie, he and his uncle Damian had stopped at the Popeye's on Tulane and Broad for a cup of coffee.

Loving a Married Man

***Conway had just graduated from the Academy. It was his first day patrolling the streets of New Orleans. The day of Conway's graduation, his mother, Bernice, had given him a Smith and Weston 9mm. Engraved on the left slide of the gun was 'Book em Yogi,' Conway's nickname given to him by his father.

Conway's first assignment was with the third district. Damian, already a veteran with the New Orleans police department, had requested that he be the one to train Conway.

Damian had been on the force for ten years and Conway only three when an anonymous tip landed in their laps, leading to the capture and conviction of the most feared gang in New Orleans.

This particular gang had been terrorizing the citizens of New Orleans known as the (E.S.) Elimination Squad. That gang was responsible for a series of murders, thefts, and carjacking's in New Orleans.

The New Orleans police force was at their wit's end trying to capture the E.S. Without help from the citizens, capturing the gang would be difficult, if not impossible.

On Conway's first day, a young man had been gunned down while sitting on his front porch. None of the residents in the area would give any information on the shooting for fear of retaliation by the E.S.

A rival gang member of the E.S. that had heard of Conway and Damian seized the opportunity to get rid of the E.S. He slipped a note in Conway and Damian's cruiser. When Conway and Damian returned to their squad car, Damian noticed the note.

The note not only provided an address, but it also gave the name of the shooter that shot the man on the porch. However, that piece of paper was not enough to bring to the District Attorney.

The D. A. would want more concrete evidence to go with that note, or arresting the offender would be a waste of time. The D.A. said, "any reasonable attorney would dispute a note without a contact person behind the note." Conway and Damian knew they would have to go rogue on that one.

They needed to gather some serious evidence to get a warrant to search or raid the Elimination Squad's hide-out. On their off-hours, they monitored the traffic coming and going from the Squad's hide-out.

They would take pictures and notes about the activities that took place. One day Damian received a call from an informant that he had helped years ago get clean from drugs.

Damian went to court to help the female informant get her children back. She had been praying for a way to thank him. When she overheard talk of a deal that was going down, she immediately thought of Damian.

The informant told Damian that the Elimination Squad had not only been dealing drugs and robbing people, but they were also selling illegal guns, and that they were expecting an illegal shipment that night.

They took that information to the District Attorney along with the name of their informant and got the warrant. That night Conway, Damian, and a swat team annexed eighteen tons of cocaine, two hundred and fifty automatic weapons, and over three hundred thousand in cash.

After the arrest and conviction of the *Elimination Squad,* both Conway and Damian got promoted to detectives.***

Conway was sitting on the passenger side of the cruiser, going over Vikki's case history. He got the feeling that Vikki and Joni were just pawns and needed to find out who the chess players were. That was the ten dollar question.

As Conway read further, he saw Vikki's mother's name was Shirley Thompson, Ms. Thompson was never married, and there was no father listed. Who was Vikki and Joni's father, he wondered?

There was something else in the

file that nagged at him. There was a Michael Duncan listed as an emergency contact. He was willing to bet his last dollar that Michael Duncan was Vikki and Joni's absentee father.

He would know who the chess players are and the reason behind the game. "Mr. Duncan, I have a feeling that you are the reason behind Vikki and Joni's kidnapping," said Conway.

CHAPTER 69

The male unsub called ahead, letting his mother know that he had retrieved the package and was on his way. He also informed Mary that the other package had been delivered.

Mary reached into her ex-husband's doctor's bag and took out the second needle that had Ketamine on it. She injected more Ketamine in Vikki's IV knocking her out cold. Again.

Not more than twenty minutes later, the male unsub arrived back at the place were Vikki was being held, shortly after two:o: clock.

He unpacked his cargo, (Joni) and threw her over his shoulder, and hauled her up the stairs. He held his nose until he got to the first room. Then he took a deep breath. He lay her on the table that was parallel to the table Vikki was on.

Mary inserted an IV needle in Joni's arm. Then she gave Joni a heavy dose of Ketamine as well. She did not want either of Shirley's girls to wake up until it was time.

Mary told her son to make sure the straps were secure. "We don't want our little movie stars to get away, now do we?

Mary started fiddling with the video camera. It had to be positioned directly on Vikki and Joni. She didn't want Shirley to miss a thing. Not one scream.

The adrenaline had been flowing in Mary's veins ever since she first saw Vikki in the lobby of their apartment building. Mary had been plotting her revenge ever since that day.

Now that the time has come, she couldn't help but fidget with excitement.
Dear God or Satan,

Wherever Michael is, please let him see what I am going to do to his precious little gals. Make sure he has a ringside seat. I don't want him to miss a thing.

CHAPTER 70

After Shirley had finished talking with Conway, she tried dialing Vikki and Joni again. Getting no answer, she began to grow restless and could not sit still.

She decided to go and check the mail to keep her mind occupied. As she opened the mailbox, a brown envelope was sitting on top of the others. On the front of the envelope, written in red, was the word, 'URGENT.'

When Shirley opened the envelope, there was a picture of Vikki lying on a table bound and sedated. Someone was standing behind Vikki, holding a brown bottle.

Shirley had to get her glasses so she could read the words on the bottle. On the front of the little brown bottle, the word, 'Strychnine' was printed.

Shirley could see that Vikki had an IV infusion in her arm. In the background was a photo of Michael. Written in red on Michael's picture were the words, 'Payback is a bitch.'

There was also a letter inside the envelope. The letter read;
Dear Concubine,

Lose something? I hope this letter finds you in the worst possible way. If not, you will be. You took my life when you stole my husband. Now, I have stolen your two Lil crossbreeds.

"As you can see, for now, Vikki is just sleeping. I gave your precious girl a substantial dose of Ketamine. She will sleep until I am ready for her to wake up.

"As soon as your other bastard child arrives, she will get her dose of Ketamine as well. At eight forty-five PM sharp, I will inject Strychnine into their IV bags. I want them to meet their grim reaper at the same time as Michael met his.

"I know, I know Michael died on October twelfth at eight forty-five AM. Well, I had planned on having your Lil pooches here at by eight forty-five AM, but Joni was not that easy to get to. Her

husband and her two Lil scruffy dogs were at home.

"I don't know if you are familiar with the drug Strychnine, but it causes severe abdominal pain, convulsions, asphyxia, and then death. I intend to make a video of them in all that pain so you can watch your girls suffer until they die.

"You have my permission to call the police, the FBI, the CIA, or even the military, but they won't find them until it is too late. Now how is that for retribution? I cannot take all the credit, though, fate played its role to perfection.

"Everything I needed to get even with you fell right into my lap. It's like your daughters' deaths, at my hands, were meant to happen this way. Farewell, you little bitch.

Your dead boyfriend's wife,
Mary

Panic-stricken, Shirley rushed back inside to call that Detective that had earlier phoned her. She could barely speak. Damian said, "Try to calm down, Ms. Thompson, we are eight blocks away."

Shirley had seated herself at her window with the phone on her lap. Calm, she was not. Finally, in a few minutes, after what seemed like hours, the cruiser pull up. Her heart began to beat with even more dread.

Before the detectives could knock, Shirley was already opening the door. She backed up a little, allowing them in. Shirley handed Damian the letter. Damian moved closer to Conway so they could read the letter together. "Damn!" they said symmetrically. "She is all kinds of crazy, huh?" said Damian looking at Conway.

Then Shirley handed Conway the picture of Vikki lying on the table with the IV in her arm and the picture of Michael in the background. "This person has my girls. She is going to kill them at eight forty-five tonight."

"Then we don't have much time, Ms.Thompson. It is already two-thirty, and we don't have a clue as to where she is keeping Vikki and Joni. That gives us approximately six hours and fifteen minutes to find your daughters.

"We need you to tell us everything about your past with Michael Duncan. We think there is a clue in your history together," said Damian.

"Michael is Vikki and Joni's father. He died when they were little. I don't think they even remember him."

"How did the two of you meet? Was he still married when you met him? Where did he work? Tell us anything that could help, Ms. Thompson," said Damian.

"I met my girls' father, Michael, at a coffee shop where I worked. There was an immediate attraction between us. He asked to take me out to dinner and I accepted. He told me how he saw me at a rally once and wanted to ask me out then, but I had vanished.

"He said he searched for months to

find me. When he saw me in the coffee shop, he said he was not about to let me get away again. At that moment, I think I fell in love with him.

"Afterward, he told me he was married, but he and his wife were very unhappy and that they never loved each other. I know men used that line all the time on women, but for some reason, I believed him.

"He said their marriage was more of an arrangement so that he could advance in his career, and she would have that social standing she craved. He'd explained to me how things worked in his world, and I understood.

"Plus, I was young, broke, and working three jobs and still could not make ends meet. Michael promised to take care of me. He said I would want for nothing. He had purchased an apartment for me and made sure I wanted for nothing.

"He must make a pretty decent living where he can take care of two homes," said Conway. "Yes, Michael made somewhere in the area of five hundred thousand dollars a year." "Wow! I think I am in the wrong line of work," said Damian.

"We had been dating for two years when I got pregnant with Vikki. He was so happy to be a father. I had never seen a sparkle in a man's eyes like that before. His wife could not have children, you know.

"A few years later, the stork paid us another visit, and we had Joni. I used to watch him play with the girls for hours after work and on weekends.

"Where did Michael work at that time?" asked Conway.

"He worked at the old Tulane Lab on Alvar street until he made a breakthrough with skin cells. Then the people at Tulane moved him to a bigger lab with a larger staff and lots more money.

"On the day he died, I think Michael was going to ask me to marry him," Shirley said as she sniffed and wiped the tears from the corner of her eyes.

"Why would you think that he was going to propose?" asked Damian.

"Michael had a close friend that knew about me named Darrell Jefferson. Darrell told me that the coroner, who was married to Darrell's sister, found an engagement ring in Michael's pocket."

"What happened to the ring," asked Conway.

"Darrell said that the coroner put the ring with Michael's personal effects. So I guess his wife has it."

"Did his wife know about the affair before the ring?" asked Damian.

"Yes. The day before Michael died, his wife came to visit me. We got into an argument."

"So she knew of the affair? How did she find out?" asked Conway.

"I don't know how she found out. We were very careful, but somehow she did. Michael's wife had threatened me the day before Michael died. She said that if I did not leave her husband alone, I would be sorry.

"I told Michael later that night that his wife had come to see me and that she had threatened me. He was very angry. I thought he was going to do something stupid. I begged him not to leave until he had calmed down.

"When Michael left me that night, he said he was going to ask his wife for a divorce. I think she killed him. She could easily get her hands on the right kind of drug to make his death appear to be a heart attack.

"Why would you think she murdered him?" asked Damian

"She's not normal. The look in her eyes frightened me more than her threats. Later on, I found out Michael had an insurance policy for me of three million dollars in the event of his death.

"That's quite a handsome policy," said Conway.

"I know, but I did not find out about the policy until he had died. The insurance agent informed me."

"When he came back the next morning, he died in my arms from a heart attack. It was strange because Michael was as healthy as a horse. And he had never come to my apartment in the morning; it was always after work or on weekends.

"I never got over his death. I am still very much in love with him. When you find the kind of love that we had, it doesn't stop at death. And nearly impossible to replace."

"You never dated any other man?" asked Conway.

"No. I did not. The pain of losing Michael is just as unbearable today as it was the day Michael died. Thank God I have my girls. They keep me from joining him.

"Was there an autopsy?" asked Conway.

"No. I always wondered whey there was no autopsy. Doctor Merrick, the ME (Medical Examiner), said that Michael had died of a heart attack."

"Hmm." When was the last time you saw Mrs. Duncan?"

"At Michael's funeral."

"Did you have the girls with you at the funeral, Ms. Thompson?" asked Damian.

"Yes, I did."

"Ms. Thompson, if you don't mind, I'd like to place your phone under surveillance. Maybe Mary will call you, and we can trace the call. I could have officers here in less than thirty minutes," said Conway.

"I don't mind. Please find my girls. They are all I have."

"We're doing everything we can, Ms. Thompson, said Damian.

While Damian was comforting and reassuring Shirley, Conway was on the phone, ordering a surveillance team for Ms. Thompson's phone.

The little worker bees in detective Conway's mind were going into double-time as he and detective Damian left Ms. Thompson's home.

Damian noticed Conway was doing

that thing he does when he is on to something. It's when Conway takes his right index finger and taps his right knee. He takes his left index finger and places the knuckle under his chin. Then he stares at nothing. Damian has watched him perform this ritual for years.

"You thinking, what I am thinking?" asked Damian.

"If you're thinking that old lab could be the place where Vikki and Joni are being held, then yes, I'm thinking what you are thinking," Conway replied.

"Since it is a kidnapping, shouldn't we call in the FBI (Federal Bureau of Investigations)?" said Damian.

"We will, but by the time they assemble a team, it could be too late. I'll make the call on the way to the lab," said Conway.

"What I don't get is why she would wait so long to get her revenge? What was the trigger?" asked Damian, scratching his head.

"I don't know unc. I just hope we

find Vikki and Joni before it is too late," said Conway.

Conway and Damian rushed to their cruiser. On the GPS, Conway typed in 2012 Alvar street.

CHAPTER 71

Shortly after Conway and Damian left, two plainclothes officers arrived at Ms. Thompson's home. One was carrying a suitcase. They were StingRay technicians on loan from the FBI (Federal Bureau of Investigations.)

The older and veteran technician, SAIC (Special Agent in Charge), Nyles Davis, was the captain of the FBI's WITT (Wireless Intercept and Tracking Team). Damian had asked for him specifically for this task.

When Damian was just a patrol officer, he had worked with Davis on a missing child case. When the department of the FBI had given up hope that the child was still alive, Davis did not.

Davis had searched for the child off-duty. A month later, Davis found the child in a little village in Mexico. He was sold to a childless couple. Davis got a promotion, and Damian was impressed.

Accompanying Davis was ASAIC (Assistant Special Agent in Charge), Timothy Adams. Adams joined the WITT team over a year ago. Adams began to explain the procedure to Shirley.

"The StingRay is a device that jams phone signals that are transmitted to area towers causing them to drop from a secure band of 4G or 3G to an insecure band of 2G," said Adams.

"Okay, I don't know what the hell you just said, but if it helps you find my daughters, then, by all means, do it," said Shirley.

While getting the water ready to make some coffee for the officers, Shirley looked out of her kitchen window. Clear as day, she could see Vikki and Joni as children playing on their swing set. They were smiling and waving to her. That was when Shirley broke down.

CHAPTER 72

Tulane University owned the two-story building on Alvar street. The businesses that rented space from Tulane were located on the first and second floors. There was a nail shop, a beauty supply store, a Radio Shack, a notary, a methadone clinic, and a clothing store.

It had been used for an array of businesses until Michael joined Tulane's team. Then the second floor had been renovated to a research laboratory. The lab was small, but it served its purpose. The other businesses continued to rent space on the first floor.

At the beginning of Michael's career, he'd managed a team of twelve employees. Among the staff was a data processor/secretary. The others were scientists and lab technicians. They worked long and tedious hours until they made a life-changing discovery.

Michael and his team had been researching skin cells. They had discovered that skin cells can be used as regenerative medicine and may cure certain types of skin diseases.

Michael and his team of scientists revealed that by implanting healthy skin on top of cancerous skin, the healthy skin would defeat the cancerous skin.

Because of Michael's discovery, Tulane Medical Center had won the Heineken Prize and was awarded handsome donations to continue studies on skin cells. And, a large bonus for Michael Which he shared with his peers.

That meant Tulane and Michael needed a bigger lab. Tulane closed down the old lab and moved it to Tulane Avenue.

After Michael's lab was relocated the businesses started to close down. The building became abandoned ever since. It had become a ghost town of space with catacombs of mildew and debris.

The trees that surrounded the strip mall mimicked a miniature forest. Wall-to-wall, homeless, drug users, and alcoholics had set up camp inside and outside of the building.

Because of its seclusion and the hazardous environment, the derelicts were the only people that dared to enter the toxic, dilapidated building located at 2012 Alvar street.

The office equipment that was left behind was now rusted and mildewed. Even the drug addicts thought the equipment was not worth selling. Wet mildewed papers covered the floors.

The building itself was rotting and decaying. Water was dripping from the walls. Puddles of water lay on the floor. Pieces of molded wood lie scattered on the floors; other pieces of molded wood leaned against the walls.

Still, it was a place to call home for the homeless, drug users, mad-as-a-hatter people, and even drifters.

All of them had been evicted.

CHAPTER 73

"It is now eight 8:0 clock, my dearest, time to wake our guest," Mary said to her son. The male unsub handed Mary two needles. Each needle had two hundred milligrams of Modafinil–the stay awake drug.

Mary looked at Vikki and Joni, waking from their nap and thought, 'I truly wished I could have been near them when they were babies; I would have drowned them both at birth.'

When Vikki and Joni started to regain a full level of consciousness, Mary introduced them to her son. "Ladies, this is my son, my pride and joy, my Avery.

"Avery! My printer! Oh, my God! I would never have suspected you, Avery. Why would you do this to me?" asked Vikki.

"You kissed Marcus! Yelled Avery standing behind his mother.

"Is that why you are helping your mother to kill me because I kissed

Marcus!?"

Avery turned his back to Vikki and faced the wall. Mary said, "Does any of that matter? In thirty minutes, you will both be dead."

"What the hell is going on?" asked Joni, still a bit loaded–fidgeting, trying to get her hands and feet free. "Why am I tied up? Vikki? Where are we?

"I remember now when I went into my garage to leave; I noticed Steven's car still in the garage. He left me a note saying he had taken the kids out for the day, so why was his car still in the garage?"

"Don't worry, ma'am; I locked them in the shed in your back yard," said Avery.

"You Lil retard. You locked my kids in the shed?"

"Yeah. But, I put your husband and your kids to sleep first."

"You drugged my children? Untie me! I am going to beat the fuck out of your stupid ass!"

"My mother said I should not untie you til you're dead."

"Dead! Vikki! Joni said, looking at Vikki. What the hell is going on?"

"These are my stalkers, Jay. My neighbor Mary Pearson and my printer, Avery," Vikki said in a conquered tone.

"Is that the Lil bastard that clogged my toilet on the 4th of July?!"

"Yeah, that's him.

"And is that the mean bitch that lives next door to you?"

"Yeah, that's her."

"What the fuck? You Lil bitch, if anything happens to my kids and husband, I will come back from the dead to fuck you and that psycho bitch up."

Mary walked over to Joni and slapped her across the face. She yelled at Joni, "shut-the-fuck-up. Don't ever threaten my son."

Now, I'm sure that both of you are in the dark about a lot of things, little girls. So let me enlighten you. Now that you know who is going to kill you, I don't want you to die without knowing why.

CHAPTER 74

"When I first applied for a condo in your apartment building, the manager was giving me a tour when you passed by. You stopped to talk to Jason about your bathroom sink being stopped up.

"You looked right into my eyes and smiled. I couldn't help but think that that young lady favors my late husband so much.

"Then it hit me! I thought both of you would be about that age now. I watched you walk away, and your figure reminded me of your mother's figure.

"No fucking way! I thought of all the people in the world to run in to. But, I still kept trying to convince myself that it can't be you. I don't think you noticed how I was staring at you, but I was staring my ass off.

"So I asked the doorman your name. Once I'd found out who you were, I was curious about you. So, I did a little internet checking, and well, I'll be damned. It *was* the grown daughter of the bitch that tried to steal my husband.

"That familiar rage started to resurface when I saw you walk across the parking lot one day. I felt an overwhelming desire to run over your ass in my car.

"Another time, you had a cake delivered to your apartment, but you were not at home. I saw it in the hallway and started to sprinkle a little poison on it, but then I thought others might eat the cake too. My beef was not with them.

"So then I dug a little deeper and got a lot of information about you off the internet, especially Facebook.

"You'd posted a picture of that tramp, your mother, and her little trampettes, you two, on Facebook. When I saw that picture on your desk at your office, I ripped it to shreds. My son did the rest to *total* your office.

"Then I began to remember that building had a history, which was why I was so interested in living there. I did my homework. You'll never guess what I uncovered. The layout of our building revealed several secret passageways.

"When I found out which apartment you lived in, I had to have the apartment next to it. One of the secret passageways was adjourned to the closet next door to you. Things couldn't have been more perfect.

"Then, I tried to negotiate something with your neighbor financially, but she was stubborn. If she had agreed to my terms, she would be alive today.

"Oh, my God! Mandy's death was not an accident?"

"No stupid, aren't you listening? It was not an accident? *Was her name Mandy? Go figure.* And that camera you had installed pointed at the living room door. Luckily for me, the closet was under the camera."

"Vikki? Mom?" asked Joni without asking.

"I don't know, Jay. I don't know."

CHAPTER 75

"**M**aybe I should start at the beginning. I can see you're somewhat confused. Your mother wasn't the shiniest light bulb in the pack either. You see, your mother had an affair with my husband. You, the older bastard child, and your sister, the younger bastard child, were the results of that affair.

"When I confronted your mother and threatened her, that bitch had the audacity to threaten me in return. Can you believe the mistress threatened the wife?"

"I remember you now. I had gotten out of bed to find my mother, and I saw her arguing with someone. You were the lady my mother was arguing with that night. I saw a lady standing close to my mother shouting. Then the woman shoved my mother on the sofa.

"My mother stood up and said something to the lady that made her so mad, she stormed out of our house slamming the door so hard behind her she knocked down a picture of Joni and me," said Vikki.

"That would be me. But, your mother wasn't as dumb as I gave credit for being. Instead of fighting back, she counted on my husband's ability to be gallant.

"I'm guessing, she boo hoo *ed* to my husband because it was that night he decided to leave me. Clever Lil bitch."

"But why take it out on my sister and me?"

"Because my little one, the way to a woman's heart is through her children."

CHAPTER 76

Conway had placed a call to the FBI with detailed accounts of Vikki and Joni's abduction. But there was not enough time to wait for the FBI to respond. Once again, Conway and Damian went rogue.

The only road to Alvar had been shut down because of a train derailing. Conway argued with the foreman who was deciding the best way to clear the street.

"There is no other way in. You will have to wait until we can clear a passage," said the foreman.

"It's a matter of life or death if we don't get through now!" demanded Conway.

"As you can see, there is nothing I can do," replied the foreman.

While waiting for a way to get to 2012 Alvar street, detective Conway began to wonder if Michael had died of a heart attack or something more menacing.

Conway placed a call to the coroners' office and requested a copy of Michael's death certificate. Then he called headquarters and requested everything they could pull up on Michael Duncan.

In a matter of minutes, the receptionists had faxed over Michael's history. The report stated his name, his date-of-birth, his occupation, where he worked, where he went to college, and other basic information about Michael's parents.

And, the Medical Examiner's report read no autopsy performed. Heart attack conclusive. However, the assistant coroner's initial report read that the heart attack was inconclusive and requested an autopsy.

Yet the death certificate read heart attack as well. The assistant coroner's report had been overruled by the CME (Chief Medical Examiner.)

"Ms. Thompson was right; there wasn't an autopsy," said Conway. How could the results be different? Conway called the office again and asked the receptionists to fax everything she could find on Mary Duncan, the wife of Michael Duncan.

One of the fax stated that Mary had been committed to a mental facility shortly after Michael's death for severe depression. "Mary is not certifiable; years ago, she was certified.

"It all fits now, unc. Conway explained. Mary Pearson's name used to be Mary Duncan. Mary remarried a few years after Michael had died. That's how she got the last name, Pearson. They had a son and named him Avery Pearson. But a year ago, Avery's last name was changed to Duncan.

"Mary was in a car accident while she was pregnant with Avery. Avery suffered a traumatic brain injury, and it left him with only sixty percent mental capacity.

"I still don't know what triggered Mary to act now. Apparently, she had been suppressing her rage for Shirley all these years for attempting to take her husband. Something happened that brought those emotions to surface again.

"But instead of harming Shirley, Mary wanted to hurt her unimaginably. Take away the two people Shirley loved most in this world, her daughters. A typical case of a woman scorned unc.

"Mary finds out that her husband was having an affair. She goes to the other woman and demands that the woman leaves her husband alone.

"And, to find out that her husband was having an affair with a black woman and that he fathered the black woman's two kids must have made her feel some kind of way.

"When the husband asked for a divorce because he wants to be with the black woman Mary was not about to let that happen.

"Ms. Thompson said Michael made somewhere in the area of five-hundred-thousand dollars a year. Maybe Mary did not want to see a black woman with the money she thought she should rightfully have. So she kills the husband."

"Vikki and Mary live in the same apartment building? Mary must have recognized Vikki when she saw her. Seeing Vikki after all those years could have been the trigger, and those feelings of rage for Vikki and Joni's mother came back. Maybe even stronger," said Damian.

"I think you may be right, unc," said Conway. In Mary's mind, the only way to get rid of those feelings was to kill Vikki and Joni. Maybe Mary resented Shirley's girls for being born healthy and her son being born mentally challenged. Who knows if we are right or not, but I think we are about to find out.

Today is October 12th. She wants to kill the girls on the same day their father died," said Damian.

"Again, you may be right unc," said Conway.

"Should we call Ms. Thompson and the baby daddy to let them know what we discovered?"

"Not yet, unc lets see if my hunch about where Vikki and Joni are being held is right. No need to build their hopes up if I'm wrong, it would be too big of a let down for them if I am wrong.

Finally after hours of waiting and pacing, the cleanup crew had cleared enough of the debris away where Conway and Damian could pass.

"Step on it, unc!"

CHAPTER 77

"Ladies, it is almost 8:00 PM. almost time for you to meet your Lord and Saviour. Any last-minute questions?

"Did you harm my mother?" asked Vikki.

"Not a bit. Your mother will be harmed enough when the police pull your dead, bloated bodies out of the Mississippi River."

"This bitch is mad scientist crazy," said Joni.

"What did you do to my dogs?" Vikki asked, trying to buy more time, hoping someone was out there searching for Joni and her.

"Seriously! You are about to die a horrible death *that I will record to send to your mother,* and you want to know about your Lil doggies?

Well, silly, I gave the little carpet shitters Acepromazine to put them to sleep. I waited until you took them out for a walk, and I spiked their dog food. Don't worry; it is harmless.

"They will wake up in a couple of days, good as new. I couldn't afford to have your Lil miniature rent-a-cops barking and waking the neighbors. That would have foiled my plans."

"It was you, the hooded person that was entering my apartment."

"Sometimes, …but mostly, it was my son. One night, I watched you while you slept and noticed how much you looked like my husband. I wanted to crush your skull in."

"Was that you or your son across the street from the camera shop?" What about the parking lot?" asked Vikki, still trying to buy more time.

"Him again on both counts. When I could not follow you, my son would and report back to me. I think he has developed a little crush on you because lately, he had been holding back information about you," Mary said, giving Avery an evil stare.

"But...How did you get in my apartment after I had the locks changed?" asked Vikki.

"Pay attention heifer!" said Mary giving Vikki a nudge against the head. "Once again, you are not listening. At first, we got in two ways. You never locked your balcony door. After you changed the front door locks, we started using the balcony until you got the cameras.

"We could not come in that way anymore. Thank God for those old mansions and their secret passageways. I didn't want to use the secret passageway at first because I couldn't have you investigating how we got in and out of your apartment without being seen. That would have changed things for me.

"This part is almost too good to believe. My son got a job with your company. I noticed in the want ads section of the paper that you needed a printer. I forged a resume and a letter of recommendation.

"Years ago, my son had a breakdown. I checked him into the Sacromb mental facility. Otherwise, he would not have learned how to use a printing machine and would not have gotten the job with your company.

"The more I think about it, the more I realize that fate put everything into motion for this day. I couldn't have planned it better. If you hadn't moved back home, I would never have seen your hideous face.

"If you had not moved into that particular apartment building, I would not have had access to your apartment.

"If Michael had not been a scientist, I would not have had the code he used to purchase the drugs I needed for you, Joni and her family, and your little doggies.

"If my son had not been an electronics junkie, he would not have been able to dismantle your peeping tom system. He rigged it so the light would stay on, and you would think it was still working. My son is so clever.

"If Michael had not kept the keys to this building, I would not have access to it, and you two would not be lying on those tables getting ready to die because I would not have a place to kill you.

"Let's not forget the nightclub you and that married man went to. I stood by your table, waiting for you to turn your back so I could spike your drink.

"For a second there, I thought you saw me put the GHB (gamma-hydroxybutyric acid) in your drink, but you didn't. You had your head so far up that married's ass you would not have noticed if God himself was in that club.

"When you got back to the table and sat down, I watched you take a sip. Then you down the drink. And I thought to myself *she's an alcoholic.*

"To be honest, in the beginning, I only wanted to scare you to death. But when I saw you and that married man screwing around in Biloxi, I knew I had to do something to stop you from being like your mother.

"I prayed and prayed for vengeance. Finally, fate handed you to me on a silver platter. I would finally get part two of the justice I deserved. Part one of that justice was killing my husband.

"Can you imagine what it would have been like for me to fall from a good society? Your friends disappear one by one. Doors closing one-by-one.

"Your standing is no longer in place. You fall to the bottom of the list like the rest of you common women. I was not born to have a common life.

"Luckily for me, I found another donor, and we had a son. My son is a few years younger than you, Joni, you know. He was born kind of wrong. I punished myself for years for his congenital disability. Then I blamed my ex-husband and your mother.

Had it not been for their affair, I would not have married Walter. I would not have been living in Gentilly estates. I would not have been driving on Louisa street that terrible day.

CHAPTER 78

Ronald and Marty had been pacing ever since Conway and Damian left. Marcus was still on the phone…waiting. "Why haven't we heard anything yet?" asked Marty. I take back almost everything I said about Vikki being pregnant for Marcus."

"They're going to be all right, boo, said Ronald holding Marty in his arms. I've been praying too." "How far along do you think Vikki is?" asked Marty. "She seems like she is about two or three months." "I got to wait six more months before I can get my drink on with Vikki again?" asked Marty.

"How do you always manage to make everything about you?" asked Ronald.

"Even longer, if she breastfeeds," said Marcus through the phone.

"Ain't nobody talking to you. This is all your fault," shouted Marty.

Marcus was too worried about Vikki to give Marty a reply. He was also pacing-praying. *Dear God, I know I don't know you very well, but Vikki does. If not for me, please, for Vikki's sake, bring her and my baby home safely. I promise to make things right.*

Marty heard Marcus praying and did not have the heart to pass a sarcastic comment. Instead, he consoled Marcus. For the first time in Marty's life, he felt someone else's pain.

He picked up the phone and in a sensitive tone told Marcus that Vikki and the baby would return home safely. Marcus looked at the phone, not believing Marty had said those words and thanked him.

"Look at you. Got a heart," said Ronald.

"It comes and goes,"

CHAPTER 79

"It is nearly 8:0 clock. It will be dark soon, nephew. Don't you think we should call for backup?" asked Damian.

"Not if my hunch is wrong, unc."

Conway and Damian had parked four blocks down in the sixteen-hundred block of Alvar in the Desire projects. The building was exactly three blocks from the Desire projects.

Spectators watch from down the street as they briskly walk toward the abandoned building. Some of the men that were hanging just outside the Desire Projects threw shade at them.

"Here, piggy, piggy! One of them yelled."

Damian stopped and turned toward the spectators and said, "Why do y'all hate the police so much? We are here to protect you all. A couple of them laughed and said, "You mean to kill us all." You could see the anger in Damian's eyes.

"Come on, unc. That's just the way these people are."

"Naw, naw, we are all being labeled as the bad guys because of what a select few have done. You want to know what *is* bad, all of you killing each other, your *own* kind, that's what's bad.

And, If you hate the police so much, then why is it when something happens, a policeman is the first person you call?"

"That's true unc, but right now, we need to find Vikki and Joni, Conway said softly in Damian's ear."

"Shit! For a second there, I had forgotten all about Vikki and Joni."

Conway and Damian rushed to the side of the two-story building. Damian poked his head around the corner and said, "Clear." Practically sprinting, they both dashed to the front door of the building. The glass door that used to be a sliding glass door was now just a glass door.

Conway pried his hands between the doors and forced it open. The smell made them take two steps backward and cover their noses. The smell of the dilapidated building was sickening.

They went into the lobby with their weapons drawn. They were relieved that they did not have ward off any vagrants.

To the left and right side of the foyer, were, what used to be, neon signs in the shape of arrows. In bold letters was the word, stairs.

The floors were littered with needles, crack pipes, rubber armbands, spoons, cigarette lighters, paper, clothing, and puddles of mildewed water.

In the center of the first floor were two large pillars. Conway signaled Damian to take the pillar to the right, and he would take the pillar to the left. They both gave each other a heads-up and sprinted towards their elective pillars.

The pillars were cluttered with graffiti. When Conway reached his pillar, he noticed, enclosed in a callout was, Johann loves Monica.

"Conway whispered, "Hey unc, I love Monica."

"What?" Damian answered, looking confused.

"Never mind."

Also, in the center of the building, beyond the foyer was a partition that separated the offices on the left from the offices on the right.

On both walls of the partition were mildewed and water damaged paintings, a direction board, and on one side was a painted arrow with the word 'east' on it. On the other side of the partition on the wall was a painted arrow with the word 'west' on it.

On both sides of the partition was a painted arrow that said 'elevator' and those pointed to the rear of the building.

Conway went to the left side of the partition, and Damian went to the right side. There was a public bathroom on Conway's side. "Why did I choose the left side?" said Conway. He carefully checked each stall, with his fingers pinching his nostrils, to make sure they were vacant.

The toilets that lined the right side of the bathroom were full of urine, feces, and vomit. The sinks to the left were stained due to lack of cleaning. The odor was so horrible that it caused Conway to gag a little.

He went down the hall room-by-room, checking for vagabonds. One room was formerly a snack area of some kind. It still had empty vending machines. Another was a beauty shop. Another was a notary office.

On the right side of the partition, Damian checked what used to be a receptionist area. It had a large window, and the door that opened the receptionists' station was locked. The lock on the door had several scratches on it as if someone had tried to force it open.

Next to it was a room that appeared to have been an office. It still harbored a few desks and chairs. Piled in one corner were broken computers, phones, and printer machines.

Down the right side of the hall, there were several more rooms. Damian walked through each of them, making sure no denizens were hiding in small places. They were all vacant.

Damian was at the other end of the hall, pointing to an elevator. Conway shook his head and pointed to the stairs at the entrance of the building. Conway took the stairs to his right, and Damian took the stairs to his left.

As they reached the second floor, the sign in front of them read 'Tulane Laboratories.' There was also a partition the separated the second floor into two sides.

The second floor also had arrows that pointed left and right, and read, east and west. Below the arrows was a direction board.

The halls of the second floor reeked as bad as the bathroom did, Conway thought. The drug users that had occupied the space sometimes did not bother to go to the bathroom or even outside to relieve themselves.

Conway cautiously walked to the left of the partition. On the left of the hall were a couple of offices and a small break room. All the doors were open and unoccupied.

Damian walked slowly to the right of the partition. On the right side of the hall were several labs and a storage room. They could hear echos of someone talking at the end of the hall.

As they reached the end of the hall, Conway turned right, and Damian turned left. In the middle was a door with a window. They both glanced into the room and saw a light coming from the room in the rear.

Behind them was a mirror. Through the corner of Conway's' eye, he could see movement. He turned quickly, ready to discharge his weapon when he saw that it was Damian and himself. "Man, that mirror almost got shot."

Conway's phone ringing echoed throughout the halls. He answered the phone in a whisper. It was Marcus. He said he was going off his trolley, not knowing what is going on.

"I'll have to hit you back, Marcus, we are checking on something," whispered Conway.

Now Conway's biggest concern was if Mary was in the building whether or not she had heard his phone ring. Time was more crucial than ever."Think she heard the phone ring, unc?" asked Conway. "Yeah, unless she is deaf."

Conway's phone rang again. It was Sergeant Archer. Conway was concerned about Joni's family. He wondered if Joni was kidnapped, then where are her husband and children.

"We got em, Conway," said Archer.

"Are they alive?" whispered Conway. We're transporting the husband and two children to University Hospital as we speak."

"Think she heard that, unc?"

Loving a Married Man

"Yep."

CHAPTER 80

Earlier, Conway had put in a call to Sergeant Archer to assemble a team and check on Joni's family. He explained to Archer that Mrs. Steven (Joni) Dallas had been kidnapped, and the whereabouts of her family were still unknown.

Archer took with him a team of seven police officers to investigate. Three Police Corporals, Sanders, Smith, and Brown. Two Police Officers, Miller and Green, and two off-duty Police Patrolmen, Berry and Moore.

Archer signaled Smith and Brown to move to the rear of the house. Millier and Green to take the right side of the house, and Berry and Moore take the left side of the house.

Archer and Sanders stood in position at the front of the house on opposite sides of the door. Archer released his 9mm from its holster, signaling Sanders to knock. Sanders released his Walther PPQ M2 from its holster and pointed his weapon in an upright position. Sanders knocked three times on the door.

"Mr. Dallas!" Archer called out. No answer. Sanders knocked again, still no answer. Sanders reached for the doorknob and turned the handle. The door was unlocked.

"That's not good," said Archer.

When Archer and Sanders were training to become police officers, they were trained to expect the unexpected. The first rule of law enforcement is for all officers to return home safely.

During their training as police officers, on search and seizure, cardboard cutouts of little children popped out from nowhere, and they shot them all.

Since the academy, they learned to think without the gunbelt. They learned to announce themselves and who they were, but be ready for anything. On high alert, after being informed that there were children on the premises, they proceeded with extreme caution.

Sanders eased the door open, took a step back, and checked behind the door. It was clear to enter the living room. Archer called out again, "Mr. Dallas, this is the New Orleans Police Department. If you are home, please acknowledge."

Getting no response, Archer and Sanders moved guardedly throughout the house. "Dining room clear," said Sanders. Kitchen clear," said Archer.

Archer moved toward the door that led to the garage. He knocked on the garage door with the butt of his gun and yelled again, "Mr. Dallas, this is the New Orleans Police Department."

Hearing no answer, Archer eased the kitchen door open while not standing directly in front of the door. Never stand directly in front of the door is another strategy they were taught.

He noticed a car in the garage. Before checking the contents of the car, he did a quick visual sweep. Realizing no one was in the garage, Archer moved swiftly to the car. Empty. "Garage clear!"

They both met up at the foot of the stairs. Continuing upward toward the bedrooms, Sanders noticed a female doll lying on the stairs with her face bashed in as if someone had stepped on it.

Archer checked Javon's bedroom. Clear. Sanders checked Lovec's bedroom. Clear. They both headed toward the master bedroom down the hall. Clear. "All clear inside!" shouted Sanders.

While Smith and Brown were at the back door, Smith noticed the shed. Smith signaled to Brown that he was going to check it out. Smith, with his weapon drawn, moved slowly and cautiously toward the shed.

Law enforcement officers know only too well how quickly situations like this can turn dark in the blink of an eye. Smith's adrenaline was causing him to sweat amply. He wiped his forehead with the sleeve of his uniform shirt.

As Smith got near the shed door, he spotted it had a lock on it. Smith used the shovel that was lodged up against the shed door and hit the lock four times.

It popped off and fell to the ground. Brown was watching for movements near and around the shed while still being watchful of anyone that may run out the back door.

Smith eased the rusted squeaky door open. There they were asleep on the shed floor. "They're in here!" shouted Smith. He rushed to Steven first and put two fingers to his neck. "The dad's got a pulse!"

Brown ran to the shed running into Joni's bird chime. Smith looked up, smiled, and said, "check the kids." Brown kneeled and put his finger under Lovec's nose. "She's breathing." He checked Javon for breathing. He's breathing. They both sighed relief.

CHAPTER 81

Conway and Damian crept inside the first room, being mindful of their surroundings. That room did not have the smell that lingered in the hall. It had been cleaned. The slightly lit room was empty except for a few broken thistle and boiling tubes that had been swept to one corner.

The curtains at the window were brand new and had that brand new smell. Other than the broken glass in the corner, the room was neat.

The second room was brightly lit. At first, Conway and Damian had heard voices that traveled down the hall. It appeared to be coming from that spot. Now, the room was quiet...

"Quiet is never good, nephew," said Damian. She knows someone is here.

Damian peeked through the glass window of the door again and quickly jerked his head back. The room was now dimly lit.

"Yep, she knows we're here."

Vikki and Joni were lying on operating tables. Mary was about to inject the IVs with the strychnine when she heard a phone ring.

"One word from you two, and you will die before your time," Mary said to Vikki and Joni.

"Mary's in there. Vikki and Joni are tied to tables with IVs in their arms," said Damian.

"Come in, gentlemen," Mary said.

Mary held a scalpel to Vikki's throat. "Stop right there! Take one more step, and I will gut her throat like a fish before you can get off one round.

"Put your guns on the floor, kick them over to me, and keep your hands where I can see them." Mary did not know Damian had a 32 Deringer on his side.

Conway and Damian placed their guns on the floor, with their hands in the air, while keeping their eyes on Mary. They kicked their guns toward Mary.

Avery was behind Mary holding Joni's IV tube and one of the deadly needles, not more than a fourth of an inch from the tube.

Vikki and Joni lay helpless on the tables. They both looked at the clock on the wall. It was now 8:40 P.M. Vikki and Joni looked at each other and mimed, "I love you, baby girl." "I love you, V."

Then Mary turned her attention to Conway and Damian, "One false move, from either of you and my son, will inject *that* needle into *that* tube," Mary said, pointing at the needle and the IV that was in Joni's arm.

There 's Strychnine in that needle. A lethal dose is only 1.5 milligrams. I have ten milligrams in that needle. So think very carefully about your next move, gentlemen.

"By the time you get to my son, he will have injected enough in the, *littlest waste of human sperm's,* system before you can get close enough to stop him. She will be dead in a matter of minutes; Mary said, pointing at Joni. Because you were so clever in finding me, gentlemen, and ruining my pièce de ré·sis·tance, you get to witness their deaths."

Conway and Damian looked at each other. They knew there was no way they could get to Joni or Vikki in time. Avery would surely inject Joni's IV, and Mary would surely slit Vikki's throat.

Conway thought the only option they had was to distract Mary longer for 8:45 to pass, and maybe, just maybe, in her anger of missing her deadline, she may drop her guard.

Damian was thinking the same thing. Damian had read some books on negotiating while in the academy: the first rule of negotiating is active listening. Even though Damian had negotiated in family squabbles, barroom brawls, and shootouts his whole career it was now that his skills were dire.

"Mary, if you don't mind, I, for one, would like to know why you want to kill Vikki and Joni instead of Shirley. After all, Shirley is the one that tried to destroy your marriage to Michael."

Vikki and Joni looked at each other confused.

"You think I am stupid like these two," said Mary using the scalpel to point at Vikki and Joni. I know you are just trying to buy some time."

"No, no, Mary. If it were me and someone came along and tried to steal my husband, the man I spent years building a life with, that would make me feel some kind of way. I can only imagine how you must feel inside."

CHAPTER 82

Damian's plan was beginning to work. Mary was listening intently. *'Only two minutes til Vikki and Joni's demise,'* thought Damian. In Conway's mind, he was saying, *'keep talking, unc, defuse the tension.'*

Damian stopped talking so that Mary can add to the conversation in her words. "I wanted to have Michael's babies. The doctors said that because I had two miscarriages, I could not have any more children."

"When I found out about these two vermins, I could not control my anger. Why would God allow that piece of shit to have my husband's children and not me?"

"That must have made you very angry. Sometimes, we all have trouble controlling our anger. I know you were happy to find out the doctors were wrong, huh? I see you have a son."

"Yes, the doctors were wrong, I do have a son, and he's perfect in my eyes.

I'll let you two in on a little secret. When I went to Shirley's apartment that night, it wasn't to talk. I went there to kill her. But, when I noticed one of the little degenerates' peeking at us, I changed my mind."

Mary was opening up. Just what Conway and Damian had hoped. Now they waited for the smallest opportunity for Mary to be distracted.

"You went to Shirley's apartment not to talk, but to kill her, but changed your mind when you saw that one of the little girls were watching you."

"That's what I said, copper."

"It must have been hard for you to walk away?"

"It was at first, but when I thought of how much more suffering Shirley would endure with my husband dying, I was glad I waited."

"Tell me about your plan?"

"I knew Michael was planning to leave me. I overheard him on the phone, making plans to leave me so he could be with that worthless bitch. He left all right. He left by my hands. I poisoned his coffee. I heard he died in her arms. Sweet!

Conway looked at the clock. It was now 8:51 PM. Mary noticed Conway looking up at the clock and turned to see what time it was. As she looked up, Damian drew his 32 Deringer and shot Avery in his hand. Avery dropped the needle to the floor and grabbed his hand.

At the same time, Conway plunged for Mary, knocking her on the floor. The scalpel slide across the room. Conway tried to handcuff Mary, but she was strong.

Mary managed to get from under Conway's grip and crawl toward the scalpel. Mary grabbed the scalpel and swung at Conway, cutting him on the arm.

As Conway grabbed his arm, Mary swung the scalpel again, this time across Conway's chest. Damian had handcuffed

Avery to the space heater and turned his attention to Vikki and Joni.

Vikki and Joni were screaming for Damian to untie them so they could help Conway to kick Avery and Mary's ass. "My sister gave you a job you Lil underdeveloped troll," said Joni.

"Think we should untie the sister's first and then call for backup?' said Damian making a joke.

Damian lost his smile when he saw his nephew was bleeding from his arm and chest. Conway, still wrestling with Mary, began to weaken.

"That's that crazy strong right there. I'm not going to try and fight her. Give me an opening nephew."

Damian aimed his weapon at Mary and waited for an opening. When Mary raised the scalpel to slash Conway again, Conway leaned back and fell to the floor. Damian saw his opening and fired one shot.

The bullet hit Mary in the shoulder, sending her backward against the wall. When Mary dropped the scalpel, it landed between Conway's legs.

Conway looked at where the scalpel had landed and said, "That was close," said Conway. A little closer to the left, and that would have ruined my dreams of becoming a father."

Damian was on his cell phone, calling for an ambulance and backup patrolman. When Damian had completed his call for backup he looked over at Joni beating the hell out of Avery.

Vikki was standing next to Joni, saying, "kick his ass!" Mary was pleading with Joni not to hurt her son.

Vikki walked over to Mary and said, "oh, now you want to beg for your child, you trifling bitch when you could have killed my sister's kids. Vikki turned back to Joni and said, "Fuck him up Jay!"

Damian grabbed Joni by the waist, lifting her off the floor, swinging her away from Avery. "Your kids and husband are safe. They were brought to University Hospital."

Vikki saw her chance to punch Mary when Conway and Damian were not looking. Vikki hit Mary so hard it seemed as if Mary went flying across the room."That's for all that shit you put me through."

Though out of breath from the scuffle and bleeding, Conway smiled at the sisters and read Mary and Avery their Miranda rights.

"Mary and Avery Duncan Pearson, You have the right to remain silent. If you give up that right, I will use whatever you say now and everything you said earlier against you in a court of law.

"You have the right to an attorney. If you cannot afford one, I will make sure I find you the dumbest, laziest, and most callous attorney available. Do you understand what I just said to you?"

"Go fuck your mother," said Mary.

"I think she understood, nephew."

Conway asked Vikki, "Bet you never guessed it was your neighbor, huh." Damian asked Joni, "your mother never dated any man in over twenty years? Think she'll go out with me?"

Conway and Damian could hear the sirens approaching. The Calvary has arrived. Conway notified Marcus, Ronald, and Marty that Vikki and Joni were safe and unharmed and that they were being transported to University Hospital.

Damian notified Ms. Thompson that he had rescued her daughters and he was taking them University Hospital for an evaluation. He asked Shirley to meet him there.

ENDNOTES

Marcus and Charlotte got a divorce. Charlotte gave Marcus full custody of his girls, Nadine and Amanda. Marcus and Vikki had a baby boy. They named him Marcus Anthony Mackenzie Jr. Marcus and Vikki got married and lived happily. Ronald and Marty became the God Parents of Nadine and Amanda.

Joni and Marty Christened Marcus Jr. I know, right! Joni got burglar bars on every window and door of her home, including the garage door.

Monique told Jeremy about her gift. Jeremy had already suspected.

Mary and Avery Duncan Pearson were charged with 5 counts of 1st-degree kidnapping on Vikki, Joni, Steven, Nadine, and Amanda. 6 counts attempted murder, one on a police officer and five on civilians, 6 counts of aggravated battery, one on a police officer and five

KAYLYNN THOMAS

on civilians, they both got life without the possibility of parole. Mary's husband divorced her.

Shirley talked to her girls about their father and went out on her first date, with Damian, in over twenty years

The definition of messy: when you willfully say or do something to someone with the intent on making them look or feel or bad.

There are three things that cause a person to be messy: miserable, lonely, and bruised.

One of the main reasons I wrote this book is so that others will stop worrying about what someone will say about them and do whatever their heart desires. People are going to talk; you can't stop them from talking. But it's only a tragedy when you let their talk stop you!

K.Thomas

About the author:

Kaylynn Thomas was born and raised in New Orleans, LA. She enjoys family time, reading, and writing books. She also enjoys long walks on the beaches of Biloxi, MS. Ms. Kay, her alias, also enjoys a good horror movie and stand-up comedies. Nothing fulfills her more than the love of her family or a pen in her hand.

KAYLYNN THOMAS

In loving memory of my mother Shirley Thompson Merrick, my brothers, Joshua Louis Merrick, Alfred Charles Merrick, my sisters Bernice Merrick Jones, Judy Merrick Lipscomb, my nephews, Lavar Thirsten Merrick, Byron Duncan, and Allen Merrick. My niece, (my mini-me), Jontia Williams, my granddaughter, Keshonda Bridges, and my grandson, Kevin L. Thomas Jr.

Gone, still loved and will never be forgotten. It's a comfort to know that they are in heaven and are on my side.

Kaylynn Thomas

I wrote this book with, Idris Elba, in mind, as the character of, Marcus Mackenzie.

KAYLYNN THOMAS

Coming soon:

Slaves With Benefits
High School With Britt 'N' Gabby
(Ninth Grade)
High School With Britt 'N' Gabby
(Tenth Grade)
Madison James' Workplace Drama'